PADDINGTON
MARCHES ON

PADDINGTON
MARCHES ON

by MICHAEL BOND

illustrated by PEGGY FORTNUM

Brought to you by
The Daily Telegraph

First published in Great Britain
by William Collins Sons and Co. Ltd. in 1964
This edition first published by Collins in 1998

Collins is an imprint of
HarperCollinsPublishers Ltd, 77-85 Fulham Palace Road,
Hammersmith, London W6 8JB

The HarperCollins website address is
www.**fire**and**water**.com

Cover illustration adapted and coloured by Mark Burgess
from the original by Peggy Fortnum

ISBN 978-0-00-779228-3

Printed in Great Britain by
Clays Ltd, St Ives plc

CONTENTS

Chapter One

PADDINGTON AND THE 'COLD SNAP'

Paddington stood on the front doorstep of number thirty-two Windsor Gardens and sniffed the morning air. He peered out through the gap between his duffle coat hood and a brightly coloured scarf which was wound tightly about his neck.

On the little that could be seen of his face behind some unusually white-looking whiskers there was a mixture of surprise and excitement as he took in the sight which met his eyes.

Overnight a great change had come over the weather. Whereas the day before had been mild, almost spring-like for early January, now everything was covered by a thick white blanket of snow which reached almost to the top of his Wellington boots.

Not a sound disturbed the morning air. Apart from the clatter of breakfast things in the kitchen, where Mrs Brown and Mrs Bird were busy washing up, the only sign that he wasn't alone in the world came from a row of milk bottle tops poking through the snow on the step and a long trail of footprints where the postman had been earlier that day.

Paddington liked snow, but as he gazed at the view in the street outside he almost agreed

with Mrs Bird, the Browns' housekeeper, that it was possible to have too much of a good thing. Since he'd been living with the Brown family there had been several of Mrs Bird's 'cold snaps', but he couldn't remember ever seeing one before in which the snow had settled quite so deep and crisp and evenly.

All the same, Paddington wasn't the sort of bear to waste a good opportunity and a moment or so later he closed the door behind him and made his way down the side of the house as quickly as he could in order to investigate the matter. Apart from the prospect of playing snowballs he was particularly anxious to test his new Wellingtons which had been standing in his bedroom waiting for just such a moment ever since Mrs Brown had given them to him at Christmas.

After he reached Mr Brown's cabbage patch Paddington busied himself scooping the snow up with his paws and rolling it into firm round balls which he threw at the clothes post. But after several of the larger ones narrowly missed hitting the next-door greenhouse instead, he hastily turned his attention to the more important task of building a snowman and gradually peace returned once again to Windsor Gardens.

It was some while later, just as he was adding the finishing touches to the snowman's head with some old lemonade bottle tops, that the quiet was suddenly shattered by the sound of a nearby window being flung open.

"Bear!" came a loud voice. "Is that you, bear?"

Paddington jumped in alarm as he lifted his duffle coat hood and caught sight of the Browns' next-door neighbour leaning out of his bedroom window. Mr Curry was dressed in pyjamas and a dressing gown, and half of his face seemed to be hidden behind a large white handkerchief.

"I've finished throwing snowballs, Mr Curry," explained Paddington hastily. "I'm making a snowman instead."

To his surprise Mr Curry looked unusually friendly as he lifted the handkerchief from his face. "That's all right, bear," he called in a mild tone of voice. "I wasn't grumbling. I just wondered if you would care to do me a small favour and earn yourself ten pence bun money into the bargain.

"I've caught a nasty cold in my dose," he continued, as Paddington climbed up on a box and peered over the fence.

"A cold in your *dose*, Mr Curry," repeated Paddington, looking most surprised. He had never heard of anyone having a cold in their dose before and he stared up at the window with interest.

Mr Curry took a deep breath. "Not *dose*," he said, swallowing hard and making a great effort. "*Dnose*. And as if that isn't enough, my system is frozen."

Paddington became more and more upset as he listened to Mr Curry and he nearly fell off his box with alarm at the last piece of information. "Your system's frozen!" he exclaimed. "I'll ask Mrs Bird to send for Doctor MacAndrew."

Mr Curry snorted. "I don't want a doctor, bear," he said crossly. "I want a plumber. It's not my own pipes that are frozen. It's the water pipes. There isn't even enough left in the tank to fill my hot-water bottle."

Paddington looked slightly disappointed as a heavy object wrapped in a piece of paper landed at his feet.

"That's my front door key," explained Mr Curry. "I want you to take it along to Mr James, the odd-jobman. Tell him he's to come at once. I shall be in bed but he can let himself in. And tell him not to make too much noise – I may be asleep. And no hanging about the bun shop on the way otherwise you won't get your ten pence."

With that Mr Curry blew his nose violently several times and slammed his window shut.

Mr Curry was well known in the neighbourhood for his meanness. He had a habit of promising people a reward for running errands but somehow whenever the time for payment arrived he was never to be found. Paddington had a nasty feeling in the back of his mind that this was going to be one of those occasions and he stood staring up at the empty window for some moments before he turned and made his way slowly in the direction of Mr James's house.

"Curry!" exclaimed Mr James, as he

stood in his doorway and stared down at Paddington. "Did you say Curry?"

"That's right, Mr James," said Paddington, raising his duffle coat hood politely. "His system's frozen and he can't even fill his hot-water bottle."

"Hard luck," said the odd-jobman unsympathetically. "I'm having enough trouble with me own pipes this morning let alone that there Mr Curry's. Besides, I know him and his little jobs. He hasn't paid me yet for the last one I did – and that was six months ago. Tell him from me, I want to see the colour of his money before I do anything else and even then I'll have to think twice."

Paddington looked most disappointed as he listened to Mr James. From the little he could remember of Mr Curry's money it was usually a very dirty colour as if it had been kept under lock and key for a long time, and he felt sure Mr James would be even less keen on doing any jobs if he saw it.

"Tell you what," said the odd-jobman, relenting slightly as he caught sight of the expression on Paddington's face. "Hang on a tick. Seeing you've come a long way in the snow I'll see what I can do to oblige."

Mr James disappeared from view only to return a moment later carrying a large brown paper parcel. "I'm lending Mr Curry a blowlamp," he explained. "And I've slipped in a book on plumbing as well. He might find a few tips in it if he gets stuck."

"A blowlamp!" exclaimed Paddington, his eyes growing larger and larger. "I don't think he'll like that very much."

"You can take it or leave it," said Mr James. "It's all the same to me. But if you want my advice, bear, you'll take it. This weather's going to get a lot worse before it gets any better."

So saying, Mr James bade a final good morning and closed his door firmly, leaving Paddington standing on the step with a very worried expression on his face as he stared down at the parcel in his paws.

Mr Curry didn't have a very good temper at the best of times and the thought of waking him in order to hand over a blowlamp or even a book on plumbing, especially when he had a bad cold, filled him with alarm.

Paddington's face grew longer and longer the more he thought about it but by the time he turned to make his way back to Windsor Gardens his whiskers were so well covered by flakes that only the closest passer-by would have noticed anything amiss.

Mrs Brown paused in her housework as a small figure hurried past the kitchen window. "I suppose," she said with a sigh, "we can look forward to paw prints all over the house for the next few days."

"If this weather keeps on, that bear'll have to watch more than his paws," said Mrs Bird as she joined her. "He'll have to mind his p's and q's as well."

The Browns' housekeeper held very strict views on the subject of dirty floors, particularly when they were the result of bears' 'goings on' in the snow, and she followed Paddington's progress into Mr Brown's garage with a disapproving look.

"I think he must be helping out next door," said Mrs Brown as Paddington came into view again clutching something beneath his duffle coat. "It sounds as if Mr Curry's having trouble with his pipes."

"I hope that's all he's having trouble with," said Mrs Bird. "There's been far too much hurrying about this morning for my liking."

Mrs Bird was never very happy when Paddington helped out, and several times she'd caught sight of him going past the kitchen window with what looked suspiciously like pieces of old piping sticking out of his duffle coat.

Even as she spoke a renewed burst of hammering came from the direction of Mr Curry's bathroom and echoed round the space between the two houses. First there were one or two bangs, then a whole series which grew louder and louder, finally ending in a loud crash and a period of silence broken only by the steady hiss of a blowlamp.

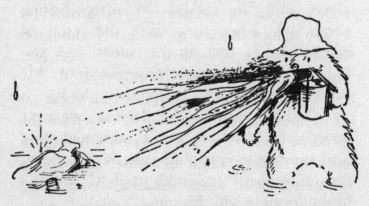

"If it sounds like that in here," said Mrs Brown, "goodness only knows what it must be like next door."

"It isn't what it sounds like," replied Mrs Bird grimly, "it's what it looks like that worries me."

The Browns' housekeeper left the window and began busying herself at the stove. Mrs Bird was a great believer in letting people get on with their own work, and the activities of Mr Curry's plumber were no concern of hers. All the same, had she waited a moment longer she might have changed her views on the matter, for at that moment the window of Mr Curry's bathroom opened and a familiar-looking hat followed by some equally familiar whiskers came into view.

From the expression on his face as he leant over the sill and peered at the ground far below it looked very much as if Paddington would have been the first to agree with Mrs Bird's remarks on the subject.

Paddington was an optimistic bear at heart but as he clambered back down from the window and viewed Mr Curry's bathroom even he had to admit to himself that things were in a bit of a mess. In fact, taking things all round he was beginning to wish he'd never started on the job in the first place.

Apart from Mr James's blowlamp and a large number of tools from Mr Brown's garage, the floor was strewn with odd lengths of pipe, pieces of solder and several saucepans, not to mention a length of hosepipe which he'd brought up from the garden in case of an emergency.

But it wasn't so much the general clutter that caused Paddington's gloomy expression as the amount of water which lay everywhere. In fact, considering the pipes had been completely frozen when he'd started, he found it hard to understand where it had all come from. The only place in the whole of the bathroom where there wasn't some kind of pool was in a corner by the washbasin where he'd placed one of his Wellington boots beneath a leaking pipe in the hope of getting enough water to fill Mr Curry's hot-water bottle.

Paddington was particularly anxious to fill the bottle before Mr Curry took it into his head to get up. Already there had been several signs of stirring from the direction of his bedroom and twice a loud voice had called out demanding to know what was going on. Both times Paddington had done his best to make a deep grunting noise like a plumber hard at work and each time Mr Curry's voice had grown more suspicious.

Paddington hastily began scooping water off the floor with his paw in order to help matters along, but as fast as he scooped the water up, it soaked into his fur and ran back up his arm. Hopefully squeezing a few drops from his elbow into the Wellington boot Paddington gave a deep sigh and turned his attention to the book Mr James had lent him.

The book was called *The Plumber's Mate* by Bert Stilson, and although Paddington felt sure it was very good for anyone who wanted to fit pipes in their house for the first time there didn't seem to be a great deal on what to do once they were in and frozen hard. Mr Stilson seemed to be unusually lucky with the weather whenever he did a job, for in nearly all the photographs it was possible to see the sun shining through the open windows.

There was only one chapter on frozen pipes and in the picture that went with it Mr Stilson was shown wrapping them in towels soaked in boiling water. With no water to boil Paddington had tried holding Mr Curry's one and only towel near the blowlamp in order to warm it, but after several rather nasty brown patches suddenly appeared he'd hastily given it up as a bad job.

Another picture showed Mr Stilson playing the flame of a blowlamp along a pipe as he dealt with a particularly difficult job and Paddington had found this method much more successful. The only trouble was that as soon as the ice inside the pipe began to melt, a leak appeared near one of the joints.

Paddington tried stopping the leak with his paw while he read to the end of the chapter, but on the subject of leaking pipes Mr Stilson was even less helpful than he had been on frozen ones. In a note about lead pipes he mentioned hitting them with a hammer in order to close the gap, but whenever Paddington hit one of Mr Curry's gaps at least one other leak appeared farther along the pipe so that instead of the one he'd started with there were now five and he'd run out of paws.

For some while the quiet of the bathroom was broken only by the hiss of the blowlamp and the steady drip, drip, drip of water as Paddington sat lost in thought.

Suddenly, as he turned over a page near the end of the book his face brightened. Right at the end of the very last chapter Mr Stilson had drawn out a chart which he'd labelled 'Likely Trouble Spots.' Hurriedly unfolding the paper, Paddington spread it over the bathroom stool and began studying it with interest.

According to Mr Stilson most things to do with plumbing caused trouble at some time or another, but if there was one place which was more troublesome than all the others put together it was where there was a bend in the pipe. At the bottom of the chart Mr Stilson explained that bends shaped like the letter 'U' always had water inside them and so they were the very first places to freeze when the cold weather came.

Looking around Mr Curry's bathroom Paddington was surprised to see how many 'U' bends there were. In fact, wherever he looked there appeared to be a bend of one kind or another.

Holding Mr Stilson's book in one paw Paddington picked up the blowlamp in the other and settled himself underneath the washbasin where one of the pipes made itself into a particularly large 'U' shape before it entered the cold tap.

As he played the flame along the pipe, sitting well back in case he accidentally singed his whiskers, Paddington was pleased to hear several small cracking noises coming from somewhere inside. In a matter of moments the crackles were replaced by bangs, and his opinion of Mr Stilson went up by leaps and bounds as almost immediately afterwards a loud gurgling sound came from the basin over his head and the water began to flow.

To make doubly sure of matters Paddington stood up and ran the blowlamp flame along the pipe with one final sweep of his paw. It was as he did so that the pleased expression on his face suddenly froze almost as solidly as the water in Mr Curry's pipes had been a second before.

Everything happened so quickly it all seemed to be over in the blink of an eyelid, but one moment he was standing under the basin with the blowlamp, and the next moment there was a hiss and a loud plop and before his astonished gaze Mr Curry's 'U' bend disappeared into thin air. Paddington just had time to take in the pool of molten lead on the bathroom floor before a gush of cold water hit him on the chin, nearly bowling him over.

Acting with great presence of mind he knocked the hot flexible remains of the pipe and turned it back into Mr Curry's bath, leaving the water to hiss and gurgle as he turned to consult Mr Stilson's book once more. There was a note somewhere near the back telling what to do in cases of emergency which he was particularly anxious to read.

A few seconds later he hurried downstairs as fast as his legs would carry him, slamming the front door in his haste. Almost at the same moment as it banged shut there came the sound of a window being opened somewhere overhead and Mr Curry's voice rang out. "Bear!" he roared. "What's going on, bear?"

Paddington gazed wildly round the snow-covered garden. "I'm looking for your stop-cock," he exclaimed.

"What!" bellowed Mr Curry, putting a hand to his ear to make sure he'd heard right. "Cock! How dare you call me cock! I shall report you to Mrs Bird."

"I didn't mean you were to stop, cock," explained Paddington desperately. "I meant…"

"Stop?" repeated Mr Curry. "I most certainly will not stop. What's going on? Where's Mr James?"

"You're having trouble with your 'U' bends, Mr Curry," cried Paddington.

"Round the bend!" spluttered Mr Curry. "Did I hear you say I'm round the bend?"

Mr Curry took a deep breath as he prepared to let forth on the subject of bears in general and Paddington in particular, but as he did so a strange look came over his face and before Paddington's astonished gaze he began dancing up and down, waving his arms in the air.

"Where's all this water coming from, bear?" he roared. "I've got ice cold water all over my feet. Where's it all coming from?"

But if Mr Curry was expecting an answer to his question he was unlucky, for a second later the sound of another front door being slammed punctuated his remarks, only this time it was the one belonging to number thirty-two.

Paddington had been thinking for some while that he'd had enough of plumbing for one day and the expression on Mr Curry's face quite decided him in the matter.

Mr Brown looked up from his morning paper as a burst of hammering shook the dining-room. "I shall be glad when they've finished next door," he said. "They've been at it for days now. What on earth's going on?"

"I don't know," said Mrs Brown, as she poured out the coffee. "Mr Curry's got the builders in. I think it's something to do with his bathroom. He's been acting strangely all week. He came round specially the other evening to give Paddington ten pence, and several mornings he's sent the baker round with a bun."

"Mr Curry gave Paddington *ten pence*?" echoed Mr Brown, lowering his paper.

"I think he had a nasty accident during the cold weather," said Mrs Bird. "He's having a complete new bathroom paid for by the insurance company."

"Trust Mr Curry to get it done for nothing," said Mr Brown. "Whenever I try to claim anything from my insurance company there's always a clause in small print at the bottom telling me I can't."

"Oh," said Mrs Bird. "I have a feeling this was more of a paws than a clause. It's what Mr Curry calls an 'act of bear'."

"An act of bear?" repeated Mr Brown.

"I've never heard of that one before."

"It's very rare," said Mrs Bird. "Very rare indeed. In fact it's so rare I don't think we shall hear of it again, do you, Paddington?"

The Browns turned towards Paddington, or what little could be seen of him from behind a large jar of his special marmalade from the cut-price grocer in the market. But the only sound to greet them was that of crunching toast as he busied himself with his breakfast.

Paddington could be very hard of hearing when he chose. All the same, there was a look about him suggesting that Mrs Bird was right and that as far as one member of the household was concerned bathrooms were safe from 'acts of bear' for many winters to come.

Chapter Two

A MOST UNUSUAL CEREMONY

One morning, just as the Browns were sitting down to breakfast, a loud rat-tat-tat sent Mrs Bird hurrying to the front door.

"I didn't want to push these through the letterbox, ma'am," said the postman, handing her two large, snow-white envelopes, "in case anything happened to them. One of them is addressed to that young bear of yours."

The Browns' postman had once got one of Aunt Lucy's postcards stuck in their front door and Paddington had given him some hard stares through the letterbox for several days afterwards.

Thanking the man for his trouble, Mrs Bird hurried back into the dining-room clutching the letters. Paddington nearly dropped the marmalade into his tea when he saw that one was addressed to him. He often received a postcard from Peru, and at least once a week a catalogue arrived bearing his name, but he'd never had anything quite as impressive before.

"Here, let me," said Mr Brown, picking up a knife and coming to his rescue. "You don't want to get marmalade all over it."

"Thank you very much, Mr Brown," said Paddington gratefully. "Envelopes are a bit difficult with paws."

A gasp of surprise went up from the rest of the family as Mr Brown cut open the envelope and withdrew a large gold-edged card, which he held up for everyone to see.

"Whatever can it be?" exclaimed Mrs Brown. "It looks most important."

Mr Brown adjusted his glasses. "Sir Huntley Martin," he read, "requests the pleasure of Mr Paddington Brown's company at two o'clock on Monday 20th February. There will be a tour of the factory followed by an important ceremony and a special tea."

"Sir Huntley Martin," echoed Mrs Bird. "Isn't he that nice man we met at the Porchester that day Paddington had trouble with his onions?"

"That's right," said Judy. "He's the marmalade king. He said at the time he wanted Paddington to pay him a visit, but that was ages ago."

"How nice of him to remember," said Mrs Brown, opening the other envelope.

"Trust old Paddington to get himself invited to a marmalade factory," said Jonathan. "It's like taking coals to Newcastle. I wonder what the ceremony is?"

"Whatever it is," replied Mrs Brown, holding up another card, "he must have known it's half term. He's invited the rest of us to see it later in the afternoon."

"Hmm," said Mrs Bird, looking at Paddington. "It's less than a week away. I can see a certain person's going to have a lot of cleaning up to do."

"Perhaps it's a sticky ceremony, Mrs Bird," said Paddington hopefully.

Mrs Bird began clearing away the breakfast things. "Sticky it may be," she said sternly. "But no bear goes visiting from this house in the state you're in at the moment – least of all to a ceremony. You'll have to have a bath and a good going over with the vacuum."

Paddington sighed. He always enjoyed

going out but he sometimes wished it didn't involve quite so much fuss being made.

All the same, it was noticeable during the next few days that he paid several trips to the bathroom without once being asked, and as a result his fur became gradually shinier and silkier. By the time the following Monday arrived even Mrs Bird's eagle eyes could find no fault with his appearance.

It had been arranged that as a special treat Paddington should go on ahead of the others and he felt very excited when he climbed into a specially ordered taxi and settled himself in the back seat, together with his suitcase, the invitation card, several maps and a large Thermos of hot cocoa.

It was the first time he had ever been quite so far afield on his own and after waving goodbye to the others he consulted his map and peered out of the window with interest as the taxi gathered speed on its way through the London streets.

On the map the journey to the factory looked no distance at all, only a matter of inches, but Paddington soon found it was much farther than he had expected. Gradually, however, the tall grey buildings gave way to smaller houses and the familiar red buses grew less in number, until at long last the driver turned a corner and brought the taxi to a halt in a side street near a group of large buildings.

"Here we are, guv'," he said. "Can't get right up to the gates, I'm afraid. There's a bit of an obstruction. But it's only a few yards up the road. Can't miss it. Just follow yer nose."

The driver paused and looked down out of his cab with growing concern as Paddington, after stepping down on to the pavement, began twisting about for several seconds and then suddenly fell over and landed with a bump in the gutter.

"'Ere," he called anxiously. "Are you all right?"

"I think so," gasped Paddington, feeling himself to make sure. "I was only trying to follow my nose, but it kept disappearing."

"Well, you 'as to point it in the right direction to start with," said the driver, as he helped Paddington to his feet and began dusting him down. "You're in a right state and no mistake."

Paddington examined himself sadly. His fur, which a moment before had been as clean and shiny as a new brush, was now covered in a thick layer of dust and there were several rather nasty-looking patches of oil on his front as well. Worse still, although he still had tight hold of his suitcase with one paw, the other was completely empty.

"I think I've dropped my invitation card down the drain," he exclaimed bitterly.

The driver climbed back into his cab. "It's not your day, mate," he said sympathetically. "If I were you I'd get where you're going to as quickly as possible before anything else happens."

Paddington thanked the driver for his advice and then hurried off down the road in the direction of an imposing-looking building with a large illuminated jar on its side. As he drew near the entrance he sniffed several times. There was a definite smell of marmalade in the air, not to mention one or two kinds of jam, and he quickened his step as he approached a small office to one side of the gates where a man in uniform was standing.

The man eyed Paddington up and down. "We're not taking on any bears at the moment," he said sternly. "I should try the ice-cream factory next door."

"I haven't come to be taken on," exclaimed Paddington hotly, giving the man a hard stare. "I've come to see Sir Huntley Martin."

"Ho, yes," said the gatekeeper sarcastically. "And who are you, pray? Lord Muck 'isself?"

"Lord Muck!" repeated Paddington. "I'm not a Lord. I'm Paddington Brown."

"'Ave you seen yourself in a mirror lately?" asked the gatekeeper. "Lord you may not be – but mucky you certainly are. I suppose you've left yer Rolls round the corner?"

"My *rolls*?" said Paddington, looking most surprised. "I didn't bring any rolls. Only some cocoa. I thought I was going to eat here."

"'Ere, 'ere, said the gatekeeper, taking a deep breath. "I don't want no cheek from the likes of you. There's an important ceremony taking place this afternoon. They're opening a new factory building and I've strict instructions to keep the gates clear. We don't want no young unemployed bears hanging about letting the place down.

"If you want a job," he continued, picking up a telephone inside his office, "I'll call the foreman. Though what he'll think of it all I don't know. It says 'Hands Wanted' on the board. It doesn't say anything about paws."

Paddington looked more and more upset as he listened to the gatekeeper. "But I haven't come about a job," he exclaimed, when at long last he could get a word in. "I've been invited to Sir Huntley's ceremony."

"Ho, yes," said the gatekeeper disbelievingly. "And I suppose you'll tell me next you've lost yer invitation card?"

"That's right," said Paddington. "I had a bit of an accident when I got out of my taxi and it fell down a drain."

"Look," said the gatekeeper crossly. "Pull the other leg – it's got bells on. I've met your sort before. After a free tea, no doubt. The only way you'll get into this factory, my lad, is through the works entrance like anyone else."

He turned as a figure came hurrying out of the main building. "Here's the foreman. And I'd advise you to watch your step. He doesn't stand any nonsense."

"There's a young out-of-work bear here, Fred," he called, as the foreman reached the gate. "I was wondering if you could fix him up."

"I told the Job Centre we're a bit short-handed," said the foreman, looking Paddington up and down, "but I reckon they must be in a worse state than we are."

"Do you know anything about marmalade?" he added, not unkindly.

"Oh, yes," said Paddington eagerly. "I eat

a lot of it at home. Mrs Bird's always grumbling about my jars."

"Well, I don't know what to suggest," said the foreman, as Paddington returned his gaze very earnestly. "Is there anything in particular you'd like to try your paw at?"

Paddington thought for a moment. "I think perhaps I'd like to see the chunks department first," he announced. "That sounds very interesting."

"Chunks department," said the foreman, glancing at the gatekeeper. "I don't know that we've got what you might call a *chunks* department. But I could start you off in the barrel section if you like. There's no one working there today.

"It's where we keep the empty Seville Orange barrels," he explained, as he led the way across the factory square past several rows of seats and a flower-decorated stand. "They all have to be scrubbed out before they're sent back to Spain and I daresay you'll find plenty of old chunks left in them if you're interested."

Paddington, who thought the foreman had said they kept *several* orange barrels, nearly fell over backwards with astonishment as the man led him into a yard at the side of the factory and he took in the sight before him. There were big barrels, small barrels, barrels to the left and right of him, barrels in front of him, and barrels which seemed to be piled almost as high as the eye could see. In fact, there were so many he soon became dizzy trying to count them.

"You don't have to scrub them all," said the foreman encouragingly. "Only as many as you can. We pay five pence each for the big ones, two pence for the smalls, so the more you clean the more you earn. It's what we call 'piece work'."

"Five pence each!" repeated Paddington, hardly able to believe his ears. He'd once scrubbed out Mr Brown's water butt at Windsor Gardens. It had taken him most of one weekend but at least at the end of it all Mr Brown had given him ten pence extra bun money. "I think perhaps I'd like to try my paw in the testing department instead," he exclaimed.

The foreman gave him a look. "You'll be lucky," he said. "You have to work your way up to a job like that. Your best plan is to start at the bottom."

He pointed towards a corner of the yard as he turned to go. "There's a brush in that bucket over there and you'll find a hosepipe in the corner. Only no playing about squirting people. There's a famous film star coming to make his footprint in the ceremonial cement today and if I catch you wandering about it'll be straight back to the Job Centre and no mistake."

Paddington stared after the foreman as he disappeared through the open gates. In the past he had often found there were days when things seemed to go wrong for no reason at all, but he couldn't remember a day when things had gone quite so badly. In fact they had not only gone badly but they seemed to be getting steadily worse with every passing minute.

He gave a deep sigh as he looked round the yard at all the barrels and then gradually a thoughtful expression came over his face. He felt sure that when the Browns arrived later in the afternoon things would begin to sort themselves out, but in the meantime he wasn't the sort of bear to let a good opportunity slip through his paws. Paddington believed in making the most of things and it wasn't often he was allowed to play with a hosepipe let alone be paid to do it, even if it was only five pence a large barrel.

A few moments later the steady hiss of escaping water began to mingle with the distant roar from the factory, and shortly after that the sound of rolling barrels added itself to the general noises as Paddington went about his task.

Several times during the next hour the foreman poked his head round the gates to see how things were going, and on the last occasion he brought the gatekeeper along as well.

"We've got a good lad there," he said approvingly. "Makes a change from some of the layabouts we've been getting lately."

The gatekeeper surveyed the small figure inside the yard. "Hmm," he said darkly. "I can see something else that's going to need a good 'ose down before the day's out." He nodded towards the factory square where a large crowd had assembled in readiness for the ceremony. "I only hope he doesn't show himself in front of that lot. Sir Huntley'll be making his speech any moment now and he won't want no young bears covered in wet chunks roaming about."

The gatekeeper addressed his last remarks in a loud voice towards the yard, but Paddington was much too busy to notice what was going on outside. Working in a marmalade factory was a lot more enjoyable than he had expected. Already most of the

small two-penny barrels had been cleaned and stacked neatly to one side and he was feeling very pleased with himself as he sat on his suitcase and made a careful note of the number on a piece of label from an old jar.

As the foreman and the gatekeeper hurried back across the square Paddington took a long drink of cocoa from his Thermos flask and then turned his attention to the huge mound of five-penny barrels at the back of the yard.

He looked up at them doubtfully. Cleaning the two-penny barrels had been fairly easy. Apart from the odd few with particularly difficult chunks stuck to the bottom it had been mostly a matter of climbing inside and splashing about with the hosepipe. But the five-penny ones looked much more difficult.

Not only were they a lot bigger but as far as he could see there wasn't even so much as a pair of steps in sight let alone a ladder which would enable him to reach the topmost ones.

Laying the hosepipe on the ground he picked up a long piece of wood and poked it between two barrels at the bottom of the pile. Things had happened so quickly earlier in the day he hadn't been able to take it all in, but he distinctly remembered the foreman advising him that the best place of all to start in a marmalade factory was at the bottom.

As he levered the wood to and fro several loud rumbling noises came from somewhere overhead. Paddington wasn't too keen on thunder and he looked anxiously up at the sky as he quickened his pace. Some of the claps sounded much too close for his liking and he wanted to get as much work as possible done before the storm finally broke.

Had he but known it Paddington wasn't the only one to feel uneasy about the sudden change in the weather. From his position on the platform Sir Huntley Martin himself cast several glances skywards as he tried to speak. Although it was a warm day for the time of year, thunder in February was most unusual and he didn't like the look of things at all.

"'Pon my soul," he boomed into the microphone. "That's all we need!"

Sir Huntley Martin was beginning to look more and more unhappy at the way things were going. The day had started badly when the famous film star who had promised to perform the opening ceremony had fallen ill, and now to have a thunderstorm into the bargain seemed the final straw.

Several times he tried to continue with his speech but each time he opened his mouth a loud rumble came from somewhere near at hand. Even the audience began to look uneasy and from her position in the front row Mrs Bird placed her umbrella at the ready.

"I wish someone would tell me where Paddington has got to," she said. "I knew he should have brought his mackintosh."

"If you ask me," said Mr Brown, "he's probably still inside the factory digging into the marmalade store."

"If he doesn't hurry up," said Mrs Brown, "he'll miss the ceremony. And he'll be most upset if that happens."

Mr Brown turned his attention back to the platform.

"If this thunder gets any worse," he said, "there won't be any ceremony to miss!"

"Crikey!" exclaimed Jonathan suddenly, pointing across the square towards the yard. "Look!"

"Good Heavens!" boomed Sir Huntley, following the direction of Jonathan's hand. "It isn't thunder at all. It's barrels!"

Everyone stared in amazement as they took in the sight which met their eyes. Several barrels were already bumping their way across the square towards them and even as Sir Huntley spoke a number of others detached themselves from the top of the pile in the yard and fell with a loud crash to the ground.

"Look out!" shouted the foreman. "The whole lot's going in a minute!"

Almost before the words were out of his mouth the rumble became a roar and before the astonished gaze of the onlookers the mountain of barrels collapsed and came cascading out through the yard gates. Most of them stopped some distance away but several bounced dangerously near to the audience and one in particular seemed to have a life of its own as it spun round a number of times

and finally ended up with a loud crash against the side of the platform.

"Mercy me!" cried Mrs Bird, as a familiar hat followed by some equally familiar whiskers peered out of the wreckage. "It's Paddington!"

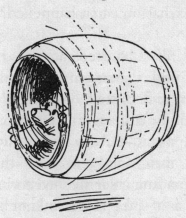

"That's the young bear I took on this morning," exclaimed the foreman with surprise.

"The young bear you took on?" repeated Sir Huntley, looking as if he could hardly believe his ears. "But he's one of my guests!

"Thank goodness you're safe, bear," he continued, stepping down from the platform. "I don't know what's gone wrong but I should never have forgiven myself if you'd had a nasty accident on my premises."

"What a blessing you had the presence of mind to get inside one of the barrels," said Mrs Bird. "Otherwise there's no knowing what might have happened."

"Oh, I was inside already, Mrs Bird," said Paddington. "I heard some claps so I climbed inside in case I got struck by a bolt."

"But what on earth happened?" asked Sir Huntley.

"I think I started at the bottom by mistake," said Paddington sadly, as he rose to his feet and dusted himself. He felt very much as if he'd been for a ride on a helter skelter, a scenic railway and a dodgem car all rolled into one, and now that he was actually standing it seemed even worse, for his paws felt as if they were sinking deeper and deeper into the ground with every step.

"Careful!" cried Mrs Brown. "Mind Sir Huntley's ceremonial cement."

"Sir Huntley's ceremonial cement!" echoed Paddington, looking most surprised as he peered down at his feet.

Sir Huntley Martin stepped forward hastily and lifted Paddington carefully out of the small square of wet concrete.

"I think, ladies and gentlemen," he boomed, holding up his hands for silence, "this is a good moment to declare our new factory extension well and truly open.

"After all," he added, amid applause, "lots of factories in the world have been opened by film stars making their footprints in the cement outside, but I don't suppose there are many that can boast some genuine bear's paw marks."

As the applause died away Paddington examined the patch of cement again with interest. "I could make a few more marks if you like, Sir Huntley," he said hopefully. "Bears are good at paw marks."

"Thank you, bear," replied Sir Huntley tactfully. "But I think we have enough to be going on with. Enough's as good as a feast.

"And talking of feasts," he added, looking at his watch, "we're already late for tea and we don't want to miss that. We've made some special new Director's Marmalade in honour of the occasion."

"Director's Marmalade?" exclaimed Paddington with interest. "I don't think I've tasted any of that before."

"More chunks," said Sir Huntley confidentially, as he led Paddington across the square towards the main building. "I'd very much like your opinion on it, bear."

Mrs Bird looked at the others as they followed on behind, picking their way through the maze of broken barrels. "I know bears usually fall on their feet," she said. "But it takes a bear like Paddington to land slap bang in the middle of a patch of ceremonial concrete."

"And get a reward of some special Director's Marmalade to test into the bargain," said Judy. "Don't forget that."

Chapter Three

PADDINGTON MAKES A CLEAN SWEEP

Paddington stood in the middle of the Browns' dining-room and gazed around with interest.

When Mrs Bird had brought him his breakfast in bed that morning he'd had his suspicions that something unusual was going on. Breakfast in bed on a week day was a sure sign Mrs Bird wanted him out of the way. But not even the distant bumping noises, which had been going on from quite an early hour, had in any way prepared him for the sight which met his eyes.

ormally the Browns' house was tidier
most, but on this particular morning the
ning-room looked very much as if a
hurricane had recently passed through. The
furniture had all been moved to one end. The
carpet had been rolled up and was standing
against one of the walls. There were no
curtains at any of the windows and the
pictures had all been taken down. Even the
grate was cold and empty and the only heat
came from an electric fire at one end of
the room.

"I didn't know you were cleaning your
springs, Mrs Bird," he exclaimed, looking
most surprised.

"Not cleaning our springs," repeated Mrs
Bird. "*Spring cleaning* – that's quite a different
matter."

"It means cleaning the whole house out
from top to bottom," explained Mrs Brown.
"It'll be your room next. We can't leave it a
moment longer."

"And talking of not leaving things a
moment longer," said Mrs Bird, as she hurried
out of the room, "if we don't get a move on
and buy that curtain material we shan't have
any dinner tonight."

"Do you think we ought to take him

with us?" asked Mrs Brown, as she followed Mrs Bird into the hall leaving Paddington to investigate the unusual state of affairs in the dining-room by himself. "He's got a very good eye for a bargain."

"No," said Mrs Bird firmly. "Definitely not. It's bad enough shopping when the spring sales are on at the best of times, but if that bear comes with us there's no knowing what we shall end up with. Bargain or no bargain he can stay and mind the house."

Mrs Brown cast a doubtful look after her housekeeper as she disappeared up the stairs. Although from past experience she agreed with Mrs Bird on the subject of Paddington accompanying them on shopping expeditions the thought of him being left in charge of the house when they were in the middle of spring cleaning raised even more serious doubts in her mind.

"I can see it's going to be one of those days," she called, as the sound of hammering came from somewhere overhead. "What with the chimney, and spring cleaning into the bargain anything can happen."

"And probably will," said Mrs Bird as she came back down the stairs adjusting her hat. "But worrying about it won't alter things.

Where's that bear? I haven't given him his instructions yet."

"Here I am, Mrs Bird," called Paddington, hurrying into the hall.

Mrs Bird looked at him suspiciously. There was a gleam in his eyes which she didn't like the look of at all but fortunately for Paddington she was in too much of a hurry to look deeply into the matter.

"I've left you some cold sausages and a salad on a tray," she said. "And there's a treacle pudding ready on the stove – only mind you don't singe your whiskers when you light the gas. And don't let it boil dry. I don't want to find any nasty smells when I get home."

"Thank you very much, Mrs Bird," said Paddington. "Perhaps I could do some tidying up while you're out," he added hopefully, as he followed the others towards the front door. "I've never done any spring cleaning before."

Mrs Brown and Mrs Bird exchanged glances. "You may do some dusting if you like," said Mrs Brown. "But I shouldn't do too much tidying up. It's all rather heavy and you might strain yourself. I'm afraid we shall have to eat in the kitchen for a day or two – at least until Mr Brown has cleaned the chimney. Though goodness knows when that'll be."

Mrs Brown gave Paddington one last look as she hurried after Mrs Bird. "I do hope he'll be all right," she said.

"Willing paws make light work," replied Mrs Bird. "And if it keeps him out of mischief there won't be any great harm done."

Mrs Brown gave a sigh, but luckily for her peace of mind, every step down Windsor Gardens took her farther and farther away from number thirty-two, for if she had been able to see inside her house at that moment she might have felt even less happy about leaving Paddington to his own devices.

After he closed the front door Paddington hurried back down the hall with an excited gleam in his eyes. There was an idea stirring in the back of his mind to do with a large interesting-looking box with a Barkridges label tied to the outside which he'd seen standing by the dining-room fireplace.

For some days the word chimney had cropped up a number of times in the Brown household. It had all started when Mrs Bird opened the dining-room door one morning and found the room full of smoke.

Shortly afterwards Mr Brown spent some time on the telephone only to announce that all the local chimney sweeps had so much work on their hands they were booked up for weeks to come.

At the time Paddington hadn't given the matter much thought. It seemed rather a lot of fuss to make over a little bit of smoke and after peering up the chimney once or twice he'd decided there wasn't much to see anyway. Even when Mr Brown dropped a chance remark at breakfast one morning about doing it himself he hadn't paid a great deal of attention.

But the news that operations were about to commence, together with the arrival of the mysterious-looking box, had aroused his interest at last.

The outside of the box exceeded his wildest dreams. Even the label was exciting. It was made up of a number of brightly coloured pictures called EASY STAGES, and across the top in large capital letters were the words SWEEP-IT-KLEEN. THE ALL-BRITISH DO-IT-YOURSELF CHIMNEY SWEEP OUTFIT.

Underneath, in smaller print, the label went on to say that even a child of ten could make the dirtiest chimney spotless in a matter of moments. To show how easy it all was, the first pictures had a small boy fitting the various bits and pieces together as he prepared to sweep his father's chimney.

Paddington felt a slight pang of guilt as he lifted the lid of the box and peered inside, but he soon lost it again as he settled down in an armchair, dipping his paw into a jar of marmalade every now and then as he examined the contents.

Although none of the pictures on the label mentioned anything about bears being able to sweep their chimneys it made everything look so clear and simple he began to wonder why anyone ever bothered to hire a real chimney sweep at all.

One picture even showed a large bag labelled SOOT standing next to a pile of silver coins and followed it with the inscription MAKE MONEY IN YOUR SPARE TIME BY SELLING SOOT TO YOUR NEIGHBOURS FOR THEIR GARDEN.

Paddington couldn't quite picture Mr Curry actually paying for someone else's soot but all the same he began to feel that Mr Brown's outfit was very good value indeed.

Inside the box there was a large round brush together with a number of long rods with metal ends which screwed together to form one long pole. Underneath the rods was yet another compartment containing a sack for the soot and a sheet with two armholes so that the person sweeping the chimney could fit it to the mantelpiece and work without getting the rest of the room dirty.

Paddington tried putting his paws through the sheet, and after screwing the brush on to one of the rods, he spent several enjoyable minutes while he hurried round the room poking it into various nooks and crannies.

It was when he decided to test it up the chimney itself that a thoughtful expression gradually came over his face. The brush went up and down remarkably easily and even with

only one rod the grate was full of soot in no time at all.

Paddington grew more and more thoughtful as he shovelled the soot into the sack and then tried fixing a second rod to the first. Although Mrs Brown hadn't actually mentioned anything about sweeping the chimney he felt sure it could quite easily come under the heading of dusting.

Number thirty-two Windsor Gardens was a tall house and as the bundle of rods by Paddington's side got smaller and smaller so the pile of soot in the grate grew larger and deeper.

Several times he had to stop and clear it away to make room for his paws as first the sack and then several of Mrs Bird's old grocery boxes became full to the brim. He was beginning to give up hope of ever reaching the top when suddenly, without any warning, the brush freed itself and he nearly fell over into the grate as he clung to the last of the rods.

Paddington sat in the fireplace for a while, mopping his brow with a corner of the sheet and then, after disappearing upstairs for a few moments, he hurried outside carrying his binoculars.

According to a note on the box lid the exciting part about sweeping a chimney was always the moment when the brush popped out of the chimney pot and he was particularly anxious to see it for himself.

Carefully adjusting the glasses he climbed the ladder which Mr Briggs, the builder, had left standing against the side of the house and peered up at the roof with a pleased expression on his face. The view through the binoculars of the brush poking out of Mr Brown's chimney pot almost exactly matched the picture on the box.

Paddington spent some time drinking in the view and then he climbed back down the ladder and hurried into the house wearing the air of a bear with a job well done. All in all, it had been a good morning's work and he felt sure the Browns would be very pleased when they reached home and found how busy he'd been.

Pulling the brush back down the chimney proved to be a lot easier than pushing it up had been and it seemed only a matter of moments before he found himself reaching up behind the sheet for the last of the rods.

It was as he disentangled himself from the sheet that a startled expression suddenly came over Paddington's face, and he nearly fell over backwards with surprise as he stared at the rod in his paw. He rubbed his eyes in case he'd got some soot in them by mistake and then gazed at the end of the rod again. It was definitely the last one of the set, as he'd counted them all most carefully, but of the brush itself there was nothing to be seen.

After peering hopefully up the chimney several times Paddington sat down anxiously in the fireplace in order to consult the instructions on the box.

As he lifted the lid he suddenly caught sight of a large red label pasted to the bottom of the box. It had escaped his notice before and as he read it his eyes grew larger and larger. It said simply:

WARNING!
AFTER SWEEPING THE CHIMNEY
GREAT CARE MUST BE TAKEN
WHEN UNSCREWING RODS
OTHERWISE THE BRUSH MAY
BECOME DETACHED!

"My brush become detached?" exclaimed Paddington bitterly, addressing the world in general as he gazed at the rod in one paw and the box in the other.

Apart from leaving the warning about the brush becoming detached until it was far too late, the only advice the notice seemed to give for when things did go wrong was contained in the four words, CONSULT YOUR NEAREST DEALER.

Paddington sat in the fireplace with a mournful expression on his face. He felt sure that Barkridges wouldn't be at all keen if he consulted them on the subject of Mr Brown's brush being stuck up his chimney, and he was equally certain that Mr Brown himself would be even less happy when he heard the news.

In fact, after giving the matter a great deal of thought, the only way he could see to soften the blow at all was to clear up some of the mess and hope that while he did so, he might get an idea on the subject.

If, earlier in the day, the Browns' dining-room had given the impression of having been in the path of a hurricane, it now looked as if a belt of thick smog had passed through as well. Despite the dust sheet everything seemed to be covered in a thin layer of soot, and looking round the room Paddington decided that in more ways than one he'd never seen things looking quite so black.

Mr Brown took his head out of the chimney and looked round at the others. "I can't understand it," he exclaimed. "That's the third time I've tried to light the fire. It keeps going out."

Mrs Brown picked up a newspaper and began waving some of the smoke away. "There's obviously been another fall of soot," she said. "It's everywhere. If you ask me, the chimney's blocked. I told you it needed sweeping."

"How *could* I sweep it?" said Mr Brown crossly. "The outfit only arrived this morning."

The Browns grouped themselves unhappily round the fireplace and stared at the pile of used matches.

"And that's another thing," continued Mr Brown. "I'm sending it straight back to Barkridges. It's filthy dirty and there isn't even a brush. You can't sweep a chimney without a brush."

"Perhaps Paddington's borrowed it for something," said Mrs Brown vaguely. "I can't find him anywhere."

"Paddington?" echoed Mr Brown. "What would he want with a brush?"

"There's no knowing," said Mrs Bird ominously.

Mrs Bird didn't like the signs of a hurried cleaning up she'd noticed in the dining-room or the various sooty paw marks which she'd discovered during a quick glance round the rest of the house, but in view of the look on Mr Brown's face she wisely kept her thoughts to herself.

"He hasn't touched his treacle pudding," said Mrs Brown. "And that's most unusual."

"Blow Paddington's treacle pudding," replied Mr Brown. "I'm more worried about the fire."

Mrs Brown opened the french windows and looked into the garden. "Perhaps Mr Briggs can help," she said. "He's just come back."

In answer to Mrs Brown's call Mr Briggs, the builder, came into the dining-room and put his ear to the chimney with an experienced air. "Jackdaws!" he said, after a moment. "You've got a jackdaw's nest in yer pot. If you listen you can hear 'em coughing."

"Coughing?" exclaimed Mrs Bird. "I didn't know jackdaws coughed."

"You'd cough, mem," said Mr Briggs, "if someone tried to light a fire under your nest. But don't you worry," he continued, opening up Mr Brown's cleaning set. "I'll have it out in a jiffy."

The Browns stood back and watched while Mr Briggs began pushing the rods up the chimney. "Good job you had these," he went on. "Otherwise it might have been a rare old job."

Mr Briggs's face became redder and redder as the rods got harder to push, but at long last he gave a final upward heave and there was a loud crashing noise as something heavy landed in the grate.

"There you are," he announced triumphantly. "What did I tell you?"

Mr Brown adjusted his glasses and peered at the round, black, bristly object lying on the hearth. "It looks a funny sort of bird's nest to me," he said. "In fact, if you ask me it's more like the brush out of a chimney sweeping outfit."

"You're quite right," said Mr Briggs, scratching his head. "It's a brush all right."

Mr Briggs began to look even more puzzled as he picked up the object and examined it more closely. "It seems to be in some sort of container," he exclaimed.

"That's not a container," said Mrs Brown. "It's Paddington's hat."

"Good Heavens! So it is," exclaimed Mr Brown. "But what's it doing up the chimney – and with my brush inside it?"

"Mercy me!" interrupted Mrs Bird, pointing towards the window. "Look!"

The others turned and followed the direction of her gaze. "I can't see anything," said Mr Brown.

"Is anything the matter?" asked Mrs Brown, looking at her housekeeper with some concern. "You've gone quite white."

"I thought I saw a chimney pot go past the window," exclaimed Mrs Bird, reaching for her smelling salts.

Mr and Mrs Brown exchanged glances. Normally Mrs Bird was the sanest member of the family and it was most unusual for her to have hallucinations.

"I think you'd better sit down," said Mr Brown, drawing up a chair. "Perhaps the excitement's been too much for you."

"It's all right, Mrs Bird," came a familiar, if somewhat muffled voice from the dining-room doorway. "It's only me."

If Mrs Bird had been taken by surprise a moment before, the others looked even more amazed as they turned and stared at the black object before them. In place of his usual headgear Paddington was wearing what appeared to be half a chimney pot which covered his ears and came down over his eyes like an oversize top hat.

"I'm afraid it broke off when Mr Briggs

poked his rods up," he explained, when the noise had died down.

"But what on earth were you doing up on the roof in the first place?" asked Mr Brown.

"I was dusting the chimney," said Paddington sadly. "The brush got detached by mistake and I was trying to rescue it."

"Paddington?" echoed Mr Briggs disbelievingly, as he began levering the pot off. "Did you say Paddington? Looks more like Clapham Junction to me. Proper mess he's in."

Paddington looked most offended at Mr Briggs's words as he sat on the floor rubbing his ears. It had been bad enough losing Mr Brown's brush up the chimney in the first place, but then to get his head stuck inside the pot and be mistaken for a bird's nest into the bargain seemed the unkindest cut of all.

"I know one thing," said Mrs Bird sternly. "You're going straight up to the bathroom. We must have the dirtiest bear within fifty miles!"

Mr Briggs gave a sudden chuckle as he looked at the others. "I'll say this much," he remarked, pouring oil on troubled waters. "You may not have the cleanest bear within fifty miles but I'm willing to bet there isn't a cleaner chimney."

Paddington looked at Mr Briggs gratefully and then hurried out of the room before any more questions could be asked. For once in his life he agreed with Mrs Bird that a nice hot bath with plenty of soap was the best order of the day.

Apart from that he had just remembered that he hadn't yet eaten his sausage salad, let alone his treacle pudding. Paddington was very keen on treacle pudding and he was anxious to make sure the cooker was turned on so that it would be all ready for him when he got downstairs again.

Chapter Four

MR GRUBER'S MYSTERY TOUR

The day after his adventure with the chimney sweeping outfit Paddington hurried down to the market with his shopping basket on wheels in order to tell his friend, Mr Gruber, all about it.

Mr Gruber chuckled as he busied himself with a saucepan on the small stove at the back of his shop. "I wish I'd have known, Mr Brown," he said. "I could have let you have several books on the subject."

"I don't think they would have helped me very much, Mr Gruber," said Paddington sadly. "It's a bit difficult reading books when you've got your head stuck in a chimney pot – especially with paws."

Mr Gruber chuckled again as he joined Paddington on the horsehair sofa. "Thank goodness the weather seems to be on the change at last," he said, looking out of his shop window as he handed over a large mug of cocoa. "I can't say I'm sorry."

Paddington nodded his agreement from behind a cloud of cocoa steam while he divided the morning supply of buns. Although he liked the winter, spring, with its promise of even better things to come, always seemed much more exciting. Apart from that, when there was too much ice or snow about it wasn't always possible to get as far as the Portobello Road and he missed his morning chats with Mr Gruber over their elevenses.

Paddington was fond of Mr Gruber's old antique shop with its rows of books and gleaming piles of copper and brass, but of late the weather had been too cold for anything more than an occasional visit. In fact the only good thing about it all was that in the meantime he had built up a big reserve of bun money at the bakers where he had a standing order.

"I've been hoping we might be able to have one of our little trips," said Mr Gruber. "Once the good weather comes I shall be busy with all the tourists and it seems ages since we went out together."

Paddington wiped the cocoa stains from his whiskers. "Oh, yes please, Mr Gruber," he exclaimed. "I should like that."

Mr Gruber looked thoughtful. "I notice a new travel firm has opened up in the market," he said. "They're advertising coach trips and they seem to do a very good Mystery Tour for one pound fifty."

"A Mystery Tour?" exclaimed Paddington with interest. "I don't think I've been on one of those before. Where do they go?"

"Ah," said Mr Gruber. "They don't tell you. That's the mystery. But they do say it ends up with a visit to a famous London landmark."

"It sounds very good value," said Paddington doubtfully. "But I don't think I've got one pound fifty. Unless they'd take buns instead."

Mr Gruber coughed. "I don't think it will come to that, Mr Brown," he said. "In fact," he continued hastily, not wishing to embarrass Paddington, "talking of buns, you've kept me so well supplied over the years I think it's about time I stood treat for a change. It would give me great pleasure if you'd come along as my guest."

"Thank you, Mr Gruber," said Paddington gratefully. "That's very kind of you."

Mr Gruber stood up and crossed the shop to his cash drawer. "That's settled then," he said, handing Paddington a five pound note. "There's no time like the present and if you've nothing else arranged we could go this afternoon. Perhaps you'd like to book up for both of us on your way home."

Paddington thanked Mr Gruber once again and a short while later, having finished his elevenses, he hurried off up the Portobello Road towards the new coach tours office Mr Gruber had pointed out to him.

The shop was called ALF PRICE COACH TOURS and as far as he could see it looked even better value for money than Mr Gruber's description had led him to expect.

On the pavement outside, a large blackboard headed *Today's Special* bore the words AFTERNOON MYSTERY TOUR – £1.50, and some of the pictures in the window looked even more interesting. Several described day trips to the seaside, others were all about coach holidays in various parts of the country, and one in particular which caught his eye showed scenes from a bumper Continental Tour called the '99 Special'.

Paddington spent some time studying the last advertisement. In fact, he became so absorbed in it he didn't notice a shadowy figure standing in the shop doorway and he was taken by surprise when the man addressed him.

"Good morning, sir," said the man, rubbing his hands with invisible soap. "Can I interest you in one of our tours?"

"Yes, please," said Paddington importantly, following the man into the shop. "I'd like two, please."

"Two?" echoed the man looking most impressed as he ushered Paddington towards a deep leather armchair standing next to a table laden with pamphlets. "Which one in particular takes your fancy? I can thoroughly recommend our '99 Special'.

"Nine different countries in nine days," he continued, brushing an imaginary speck of dust from the arm of Paddington's chair. "And you need never get out of the coach. The normal price is a hundred pounds, but I'm sure we could arrange special all-in bear rates if you're having two."

"*A hundred pounds!*" exclaimed Paddington in alarm. "But I only wanted two one pound fifty ones for the afternoon Mystery Tour."

The smile disappeared as if by magic from the man's face as he stared at Paddington's five pound note. "'Ere," he said nastily. "Are you taking the micky?"

"No," said Paddington earnestly. "Only Mr Gruber. And I'm not taking him. He's taking me because it's his treat."

The man took a deep breath and disappeared behind the counter. "I'll trouble you to get out of that armchair," he said nastily. "It's a new one and we don't want to get no nasty stains on it.

"Here you are," he continued, handing Paddington two tickets in exchange for the five pound note. "Coach leaves at two o'clock sharp. And here's your two pounds change."

"Two pounds!" exclaimed Paddington, staring at the two coins in his paw. "I think you've made a mistake."

"A mistake?" repeated the man. "Two tickets at one pound fifty is three pounds. Three pounds from five pounds is two pounds."

"But it says outside your trips are half price," replied Paddington hotly.

"Half price?" echoed the man. "Just you show me where, young feller me bear."

Paddington hurried out of the shop and pointed to the sign over the door. "There you are!" he exclaimed.

The man stared up at the notice for a moment and then back at Paddington. "'Ere, Alf," he called, putting his head inside the shop door. "There's a young bear out here taking your name in vain."

"That isn't *half* price," he said, turning back to Paddington. "That's Alf Price of Alf Price Coach Tours. He's the owner. And if you want my advice you'll be on your way before he comes out. Very sensitive is Alf."

Paddington gave the man a long, hard stare and then beat a hasty retreat in the direction of Windsor Gardens, casting some anxious glances over his shoulder as he hurried along clutching the two coach tickets tightly in his paw in case anything else happened.

"99 Special' indeed!" said Mrs Brown, when he told the others all about the morning's events. "It ought not to be allowed. Trying to get their hands on a young bear's savings like that."

"Hmm," said Mrs Bird. "I don't think we need have any worries on that score. Anyone who gets their hands on that bear's savings deserves every penny. It's what I'd call earning money the hard way."

Paddington looked most offended at Mrs Bird's remarks as he hurried upstairs in order to get ready for his outing. All the same, there were so many preparations to make he soon forgot about his nasty experience in the coach office and by the time the afternoon arrived he was looking unusually spick and span as he made his way back down the Portobello Road.

Paddington always enjoyed an outing and it was with an air of excitement that he climbed into the waiting coach and settled himself comfortably in the front seat alongside Mr Gruber.

Mr Gruber had brought several guide books with him and as they sped through the London streets he pointed out a number of the more important landmarks, explaining all about them as they came into view.

The time passed quickly, but after they had been travelling for about an hour Mr Gruber began to look thoughtful. "Do you know, Mr Brown," he said, studying a map as they turned a corner and began to slow down. "I have a feeling you're in for a nice surprise. I do believe we're going to visit somewhere very unusual."

Before Mr Gruber had time to explain matters any further the coachdriver began marshalling his passengers out on to the pavement and then led them towards a large building standing to one side of a busy main street.

Mr Gruber paused just inside the entrance in order to buy a guide book and while he was waiting Paddington stood politely to one side and gazed around with interest.

While he was looking he suddenly caught sight of a small kiosk standing nearby and an excited gleam came into his eyes as he took in the display of brightly coloured postcards on the counter, several of which showed views of sights they had passed that very afternoon.

Paddington had enjoyed his outing no end and knowing Mr Gruber's fondness for pictures it seemed a good chance to repay him for some of his kindness.

Carefully making sure no one was watching, Paddington took some money out of the secret compartment in his suitcase and then hurried across the hall.

"I'd like two large souvenir postcards, please," he announced, tapping importantly on the counter. "Some of the special coloured ones."

Being rather short Paddington was used to having trouble with counters, but even he began to get more and more impatient as the lady in the kiosk stared with a fixed expression on her face at some distant object above his head. He looked round anxiously as the coach party began moving forward towards some stairs at the back of the hall and several times he gave the figure behind the counter some extra hard stares, but for once the ones he got back in return seemed harder still.

"I was going to buy some souvenirs," he explained, as Mr Gruber came hurrying up to see what was the matter. "But I can't make anyone hear."

Mr Gruber looked rather upset. "Oh dear, Mr Brown," he said. "I doubt if you will. I think she's made of wax."

Paddington peered over the edge of the counter. "Made of wax!" he exclaimed hotly. "I've never heard of anyone being made of wax before."

Mr Gruber chuckled. "You'll find a lot of people like that in here, Mr Brown," he said. "This is Madame Tussaud's. It's a waxworks museum. This must be one of their little jokes. I think the real lady's over there."

Mr Gruber pointed towards the other end of the counter as he went on to explain all about the museum. "They not only have models of all the famous people in history," he said, handing the girl some money in exchange for two postcards, "they have lots of other figures made of wax as well. Some of them are so lifelike it's difficult to tell whether they're real or not. I'm sure you're not the first one to be caught napping, Mr Brown."

Paddington listened carefully as he followed Mr Gruber towards the crowd on the stairs. Now that matters had been explained to him he began to notice quite a few figures standing motionless in the hall. Near the entrance there was an unusually still-

looking policeman, and halfway up the stairs stood another man in uniform with his hand outstretched in front of him, looking for all the world like one of the statues Mr Gruber had pointed out on their trip.

"I think we must have picked the wrong day, Mr Brown," said Mr Gruber, breaking into his thoughts. "Half London seems to be in front of us."

Paddington gasped his agreement as Mr Gruber disappeared in a flurry of people. From where he was standing it felt very much as if the other half of London was behind him as well, and to make matters worse he'd just made the unhappy discovery that a half opened bar of chocolate he'd brought in case of an emergency was beginning to melt in his paw with the heat.

Although he often got himself into a mess Paddington was a tidy-minded bear and he looked round for somewhere to put the sticky remains before too much of it dripped on to the floor. By now the crowd was too thick to lift his hat let alone open his suitcase, and he was just giving up hope of ever finding anywhere to leave it when he found himself standing next to the figure in uniform he'd noticed earlier.

Without waiting to consider the matter Paddington pressed the ball of chocolate into the outstretched hand and then turned to look for Mr Gruber. As he did so a loud voice rang out over the noise of the crowd.

"'Ere!" cried the voice. "Who did this?"

Paddington turned and then nearly jumped out of his skin as he caught sight of the man in uniform holding up a chocolate-covered hand for everyone to see.

The man gazed at Paddington suspiciously. "Is this yours, bear?" he said.

"I thought you were a waxwork," exclaimed Paddington, looking most upset. He stared round desperately for help but Mr Gruber was nowhere to be seen.

"Oi!" shouted the man. "Come back! Stop that bear!"

But Paddington was halfway down the stairs. He didn't like the look of things at all. Already several of the doorkeepers were looking in his direction and as he squeezed his way past the people trying to get up he peered round anxiously for somewhere to hide.

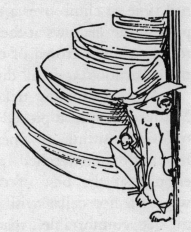

Holding on tightly to his suitcase he hurried across the hall in the direction of some more stairs. The voice of the man in uniform was getting louder and louder and there wasn't time to read the words over the opening, but it seemed the only spot left where there was no one to bar his way.

When he reached the bottom of the stairs Paddington found himself in a large room rather like a dungeon. It was much darker than it had been in the other part of the building but as far as he could make out he was standing in a long stone corridor which had a line of smaller rooms opening out along one side, each of which contained a number of figures.

The voices behind him were getting nearer with every passing second and he just had time to climb over a chain and take up a pose in the shadows at the back of one of the rooms when a crowd of officials rushed into the cellar looking in all directions.

As the minutes ticked by Paddington began to wish he'd picked a lying down pose, or even a sitting up one. Standing on one leg with outstretched paws was difficult enough at the best of times, but when it was in a hot cellar with no time in which to get comfortable, matters became very difficult indeed.

At long last the shouting died away amid a clatter of feet as the men disappeared back up the stairs. Paddington heaved a sigh of relief but before he had time to blink, let alone move his paws, some new voices broke the silence which followed. They got nearer and nearer until suddenly they stopped opposite his room.

"It says Charlie Peace in the catalogue," announced a man's voice. "But I never thought he had fur."

"If that's Charlie Peace," replied a woman, "I'm the Queen of Sheba. Besides, where's 'is number? All the rest 'ave got numbers."

"Perhaps it's a friend," said a child's voice.

"'Orrible," complained the woman. "They all look as bad as one another to me. Don't know which is worse. I shouldn't look if I were you, Lil."

"Horrible it may be," interrupted the man. "But it's very lifelike. Fancy making all them whiskers out of wax. It's a wonder they don't drop off with the heat."

Paddington opened his eyes and stared at the group outside the room. He was getting a bit fed up with the way things were going. More and more people were joining the party with every passing moment and by now the corridor was crowded with curious onlookers. It all seemed a great deal of fuss and bother to get into simply because he'd wanted to get rid of some chocolate remains.

"Charlie Peace!" he exclaimed, raising his hat. "I'm not Charlie Peace. I'm Paddington Brown from Darkest Peru!"

If Paddington had been surprised when the man on the stairs had sprung to life his audience in the cellar seemed even more taken aback at the sudden turn of events.

When he caught sight of the look on their faces Paddington closed his eyes and gave several hurried snores as he took up his pose again, but it was already much too late. The air was filled with cries of alarm from the ones in the front row and a buzz of excited conversation from those at the back who were straining to see what was going on.

Just as the noise began to reach its height the sound of heavy boots added itself to the general hubbub and a moment later Paddington felt a heavy hand on his shoulder.

"Got you!" said a triumphant voice. "If I'm not mistaken you're the young bear what mistook me for a dustbin on the stairs."

Paddington opened his eyes and looked up at the dark blue uniform. "I didn't know you were real," he explained. "I only wanted to get rid of my chocolate remains."

"Fifty years I bin here, man and boy," said the man bitterly, holding up his hands for everyone to see, "and never 'ad a bear's remains deposited on me before. We'll 'ave to see what the manager's got to say about this little matter. I daresay he'll want to take down your particulars."

"Take down my particulars!" exclaimed Paddington, looking more and more upset.

"That's what I said," remarked the man. "I don't know about 'is being a Charlie Peace," he continued, addressing the crowd in reply to someone's question. "He's a *disturber* of the peace all right."

While the man was talking, Paddington got down on his paws and knees and pulled

his hat well down over his head. A few seconds later the sound of shouting broke out once more in Madame Tussaud's, only this time it was directed towards the stairs as a small brown figure disappeared up them as fast as its legs would go. Paddington believed in getting his money's worth, but he'd had quite enough adventures for one day, even for a one pound fifty bargain mystery tour.

"Thank goodness we bumped into each other when we did," said Mr Gruber later that afternoon as they sat in his shop having tea. "I looked everywhere for you, but I must say it didn't occur to me to try the Chamber of Horrors."

Mr Gruber chuckled as Paddington went through his adventure once again. "They must have been surprised when you raised your hat, Mr Brown," he said. "I expect they thought you were one of the horrors!"

Mr Gruber coughed and hurriedly changed the subject in case he'd said anything to offend, but Paddington was much too busy staring out of the shop window to notice anything amiss.

He'd just caught sight of a newspaper boy going past with a placard over his arm and across it in large, black letters were the words WAXWORKS MUSEUM LATEST – MYSTERY DEEPENS!

The boy was too far away for him to see the actual papers clearly but one of the headlines definitely had the word BEAR in it.

"Good gracious," exclaimed Mr Gruber, as he followed the direction of Paddington's gaze. "I think we'd better buy a copy, Mr Brown. In fact, we'd better buy several copies. I can think of quite a lot of people who'll want one as a souvenir and you'll certainly need an extra one for your scrap book.

"After all," he added, as Paddington hurried out of the door, "lots of people go on mystery tours, but not many can say they've actually *taken* part in one let alone been able to read about it when they've got home."

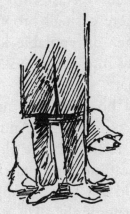

Chapter Five

PADDINGTON SAVES THE DAY

"It's all highly irregular," said Jonathan's headmaster, as he addressed the small group of people standing on the cricket pitch. "He's not even an old bear let alone an old boy."

He looked distastefully towards the boundary where a small brown figure in an odd and rather disreputable-looking hat sat dipping a paw into what looked like a large earthenware jar.

"The old boys *are* one man short, sir," said the sportsmaster. "And the crowd's getting a bit restive. If we don't start soon there won't be time for a match at all."

"We could ask him, I suppose," said the headmaster grudgingly. "He might not want to play, of course," he added, brightening slightly at the thought. "He looks very comfortable where he is."

"Oh, he will," said Jonathan loyally. "Old Paddington likes anything new and he's never played cricket before."

"We can but try," said the sportsmaster, interrupting hastily as he led the way across the field. "After all, nothing ventured – nothing gained."

As organiser-in-chief of the afternoon's cricket match in aid of the new school pavilion the sportsmaster wore a worried look on his face. In the beginning it had promised to be a particularly enjoyable occasion. A team of old boys, captained by Mr Brown, had challenged a team from the sixth form, and no less a person than Mr Alf Duckham, the famous England cricketer, had agreed to act as umpire.

Viewing the large crowd that had turned up to see the event the sportsmaster had had high hopes of raising a lot of money and the last minute news that the old boys were one player short had come as a bitter blow. Like a drowning man clutching at a straw he had eagerly seized on Jonathan's suggestion that Paddington might like to turn out for the game, but as they neared the boundary line even he began to have second thoughts on the matter.

Paddington looked most surprised when he saw the party approaching his deck chair. After the first excitement of arriving at Farrowfield had died down he'd been glad of the chance to sit down and rest. Although it was only Jonathan's first term at his father's old school Paddington's fame had gone before him and his paws felt quite limp after all the shaking and making marks in autograph books they had done. Apart from that he was beginning to feel the effects of several visits to the school tuck shop, not to mention two extra large helpings of suet pudding which he'd eaten at lunch.

"How do you do, bear," said the headmaster, taking hold of Paddington's outstretched paw rather gingerly.

"Very well, thank you," replied Paddington politely, raising his hat with his other paw.

The headmaster returned Paddington's gaze doubtfully. It was a warm afternoon and there were a number of very odd and sticky looking stains about Paddington's person, as well as some old suet pudding crumbs, which he didn't like the look of at all.

"Er… we were wondering if you'd care to turn out for the old boys this afternoon," he said gruffly.

"Turn out for the old boys?" exclaimed Paddington, looking even more surprised.

"They're one man short in their team," explained Jonathan.

"Ooh, yes please," said Paddington eagerly. "I think I should like that. I've never played cricket before."

"Eureka!" cried the sportsmaster, slapping him on the back.

"What!" exclaimed Paddington hotly, as he staggered forward. "I reeka! But I had a bath yesterday."

"It's all right, Paddington," said Jonathan hastily, as the sportsmaster jumped back looking most confused. "He didn't mean you smell. It's a Greek word. It means… er…"

"Well, Brown," said the headmaster sternly. "What does it mean?"

"Er… it means we're all very pleased he can play, sir," said Jonathan brightly.

Mr Alf Duckham gave a cough from somewhere at the back of the group. "Perhaps we'd better toss up to see who's going in first," he said, taking a coin from his pocket. "Would you care to do it, bear?"

"Thank you very much, Mr Duckham," said Paddington gratefully. "It's a bit difficult with paws but I'll have a go."

While the others stood back and watched, Paddington took the coin and after placing it carefully on top of one of his paws gave it a quick flick.

"A very good toss, bear," said Alf Duckham approvingly, as he bent down and peered at the ground. "Quite professional. Now all we have to do is find it again."

"It must be *somewhere*," said the headmaster crossly a moment or so later as he got down on his hands and knees and joined the others on the grass.

"It's all right," cried Paddington suddenly, when the excitement was at its height. "I've got it. It was stuck to my paw by mistake."

"Stuck to your paw by mistake," repeated the headmaster, breathing heavily. "Am I hearing right?"

"I'm afraid I had some marmalade on it," explained Paddington, holding up his paw for everyone to see. "I forgot to wipe it off after breakfast."

"I think," said the sportsmaster tactfully, as a loud snort came from the headmaster's direction, "we'd better adjourn to the pavilion and make a start. Though where we're going to find any pads to fit," he added, taking a closer look at Paddington, "is quite another matter."

If anything the sportsmaster looked even more worried than he had done a few minutes before. He had a nasty feeling in the back of his mind that if there was one thing worse than having a team of only ten old boys it might well prove to be that of having a team made up of ten old boys plus a young bear into the bargain.

The Browns sat in a glum group on the boundary. Things were beginning to look very black indeed for the old boys in their match against the school.

Farrowfield had batted first and by the middle of the afternoon they had declared, leaving their opponents one hundred and fifty runs to score in a little over two hours. Now, with less than twenty minutes to go, wickets were falling fast and furiously and a number of the spectators were already beginning to leave the ground. Even Mrs Bird, who knew less about cricket than any of them, could see that things were far from well.

"Perhaps Paddington will be able to score a few," she remarked hopefully, as she looked up from her knitting.

"What, with over twenty needed?" said Jonathan. "He's last man in. The old boys don't stand a chance."

With both Paddington and his father in the old boys' team Jonathan wasn't quite sure which side to applaud, but even he managed to raise a genuine groan a few minutes later as yet another loud "Howzat" from the field was followed by a burst of clapping from the school supporters.

"Crikey! That's it!" he exclaimed. "There goes Dad's wicket. It's Paddington's turn now. Seventeen needed and only fifteen minutes to go."

"Oh dear," said Mrs Brown nervously. "I do hope he doesn't stand in the way of the ball. It looks very hard to me."

"Don't worry," replied Jonathan ominously. "It's 'Smasher' Knowles, the Demon bowler of the Upper Sixth. He's a nasty piece of work. Nobody likes him but he's a jolly fast bowler. Paddington won't even see the ball."

"There he is now," said Mrs Brown, as a familiar figure came hurrying down the pavilion steps and another much louder burst of applause went round the ground.

"I do wish he wouldn't insist on wearing that old hat of his," said Mrs Bird. "I'm sure it isn't quite the thing in an old boys' cricket match."

"Best of luck, Paddington," said Mr Brown, as he met him on the way in. "Now, don't forget, watch the ball – and whatever you do, keep a straight bat. And have a good look round the field. See where the captain's placed his men. There's a silly mid-off and he's got a short leg."

Paddington began to look more and more confused as he listened to Mr Brown's advice and he nearly fell over backwards at the last piece of information.

"What!" he exclaimed, looking round at the other players with interest. "The silly mid-off's got a short leg?"

Mr Brown opened his mouth as if he was about to say something but changed his mind. "Good luck!" he called as Paddington hurried off in the direction of the wicket with a determined expression on his face.

"Say when you're ready, bear," said Alf Duckham encouragingly, as Paddington took his guard at the wicket.

"I think I'm all right, Mr Duckham," said Paddington doubtfully, looking round the field.

All in all, Paddington didn't think much of cricket as a game. He had spent over two hours in the field when the other side had been batting and the ball had only come near him twice. The first time it had been so far over his head he'd hardly been able to see it, and the second time it had taken him completely by surprise when it had landed in his lap while he was busy testing a jar of marmalade.

Despite several pleas from the older spectators that he'd managed to get a paw to it, Alf Duckham had been forced to say that it wasn't really a catch and Paddington had been most upset.

Now that he was actually standing at the wicket he was beginning to have second and even third thoughts on the subject.

Everything looked much bigger than it had done from the pavilion. There were far too many people standing nearby ready to catch him out for his liking, and when he caught sight of the expression on 'Smasher' Knowles's face as he stood fingering the ball he felt even less keen on the whole affair.

Paddington crouched down and as the Demon bowler of the Upper Sixth thundered down the pitch towards him he hurriedly filled the gap between his pads with the bat and closed his eyes while he waited for the worst to happen.

'Smasher' Knowles stopped in his run. "I can't bowl if he hides behind his pads," he exclaimed crossly. "I can't even see the batsman let alone the wicket."

Alf Duckham signalled the bowler back to his place. "Everyone has their own way of playing the game," he said sternly. "This young bear is entitled to his."

Unaware of the reason for the delay the Browns sat anxiously watching the events on the field as the bowler turned and once again hurled himself down the pitch towards Paddington.

"He looks in a jolly bad temper," said Jonathan. "This is it."

"I can't watch," said Mrs Bird. "I know something awful's going to happen."

Just as Mrs Bird closed her eyes there was a loud click of a ball hitting wood and a roar of surprise swept round the ground. "Good Heavens!" cried someone behind her. "That young bear's hit a six. Bravo!"

Everyone rose to their feet and stared in amazement at the sight of the ball soaring over the heads of the crowd on the far side of the field. It had taken everyone completely by surprise and for some odd reason even the fieldsmen were looking in the wrong direction.

Paddington, as he picked himself up from the ground, looked the most surprised of all. Apart from feeling as if he'd been kicked by a mule he wasn't at all sure what had happened, but a pleased expression came over his face as he listened to the applause and he raised his hat several times to the crowd.

"He's got his bat the wrong way round," yelled 'Smasher' Knowles, pointing an accusing finger at Paddington. "How can you tell where the ball's going if he doesn't hold his bat properly? It might go anywhere."

Alf Duckham scratched his head. "I don't know that there's anything in the rules saying you *must* hit the ball with the flat side of the bat," he said. "Can't say as I've ever come across it before. I think we'd best play on."

'Smasher' Knowles glared at Paddington and then turned and made his way back up the pitch. "He didn't even hit the ball," he grumbled. "I hit the bat!"

"Two more balls to this over," said Jonathan. "I wonder if Paddington can hold out?… Crikey!" he exclaimed, jumping to his feet again as another burst of applause swept the ground. "A four! Good old Paddington!"

Even Mrs Bird was sitting on the edge of her chair with excitement at the sudden change in the game. "He can't possibly do it again," she exclaimed, as 'Smasher' Knowles turned to make his run for the last ball of the over.

"He jolly well has," cried someone over the applause. "Another four! Fourteen off one over. Bravo bear! Best innings of the day."

"There's just time for two more overs," said Jonathan excitedly, as he looked at the pavilion clock. "And the old boys only need three runs to win. If the other chap can keep the bowling away from Paddington they stand a chance."

"I'm sure Paddington could hit another of those fours," said Mrs Bird vaguely. "He seems very good at those."

"It's old Parkinson bowling now," said Jonathan. "He's a spin bowler. Even Paddington won't get any fours off him."

The crowd relaxed as the field settled down and the bowler ran up to deliver the first ball of the over. Gradually an air of gloom descended once again as Paddington's partner made a wild swing at the first four balls and missed them completely.

"I *know* Paddington could do better," said Mrs Brown.

"He's hit one," cried Jonathan excitedly. "Come on Paddington – run!"

The crowd watched with bated breath as the two figures ran between the wickets. Paddington seemed to be having some kind of trouble with his pads and he was still only halfway down the pitch when his partner was safely home. Paddington's pads had been something of a problem right from the start. Bears' legs being rather short there had been none of the right size and in the end the sportsmaster had trimmed the ends off an old pair he'd found in the pavilion. But even so they were far from satisfactory and the tops flapped up and down banging Paddington on his knees as he struggled to make his run.

"Whew!" said Jonathan, sinking back to the ground as Paddington reached his crease in the nick of time. "That was a near thing. Two more wanted to win."

"Mercy me," said Mrs Bird. "I've dropped all my stitches."

"Best of luck, bear," whispered Alf Duckham, as Paddington took up his position. "And be careful. It's young Parkinson bowling. They tell me he comes from Australia so watch his googlies."

"Watch his googlies?" repeated Paddington, peering down the pitch with interest as the bowler ran towards him. "How do you do," he called out, raising his hat politely. "I'm Paddington Brown and I come from Darkest Peru."

The crowd fell silent as the ball left the bowler's hand and then a murmur of surprise went round the ground.

"That's funny," said Jonathan. "What's happened to it?"

Everyone craned their necks in an effort to see what was going on as first the fieldsmen and then Alf Duckham began searching the ground round the wicket.

"It must be somewhere," said Alf Duckham. "A ball can't just disappear into thin air. Any idea where you hit it, bear?"

Paddington reached up and felt the top of his head. "I don't think I did hit it, Mr Duckham," he said vaguely. "I think it must have hit me. I've got a bruise under my hat."

"A bruise under your hat?" repeated Alf Duckham, looking most concerned. "Here, let me see."

As he felt under Paddington's hat a strange look came over Alf Duckham's face. "That isn't a bruise," he exclaimed, withdrawing his hand. "It's the ball!"

"Oh dear," said Paddington. "It must have gone inside my hat by mistake when I raised it just now."

Alf Duckham took a deep breath. "End of the over," he called, signalling the players to change sides again.

"That's torn it," groaned Jonathan. "Trust old Paddington to do a thing like that. Now there's only time for one over and it's 'Smasher' Knowles's turn again."

"And they say cricket's a dull game," exclaimed Mrs Bird.

"Not when Paddington's playing," said Mr Brown. "If only they can get another two runs." Mr Brown stood with his hands ready to applaud as play began but they got noticeably lower and lower as first one ball and then another whistled past Paddington's partner untouched by the bat.

"Last ball of the day coming up," he groaned. "He must hit this one."

"He has too!" cried Jonathan, as a loud click came from the field. "Come on, Paddington – run. One more for a tie – two for a win!"

Other voices added themselves to Jonathan's and within a matter of moments the whole ground was in an uproar. From his position in the centre of the pitch Paddington struggled on oblivious to it all. Amongst the general hubbub he could vaguely catch the sound of his name and he remembered seeing his partner pass him several times going in opposite directions, but he was much too busy trying to stand up let alone run as his pads slipped lower and lower down his legs. Once he even felt someone pick him up and point him in the right direction but beyond that everything seemed like a bad dream as he tried to move his legs and nothing happened. No one on the field was more surprised than he was when at long last the wickets loomed up ahead and he found himself safely home.

"Well," said Mrs Brown. "What happens now? Paddington's run one and his partner's run three."

"It'll be a tie," said Mr Brown. "They'll just have to count Paddington's one."

But on the field Alf Duckham, entering into the spirit of the game, was having different ideas on the subject.

"I think," he announced, holding up his hand for silence, "in view of all the circumstances, we'll award the old boys one and a half runs and give them the game."

Mr Duckham's announcement was greeted by a storm of applause from spectators and players alike, and even 'Smasher' Knowles was seen to be clapping with the rest.

"Hear! Hear!" echoed the headmaster, as he came on to the field. "A very fair decision. A trifle unusual and not quite in the book of rules. But very fair."

The headmaster of Farrowfield looked very pleased with himself at the unexpected success of the day's activities. The excitement towards the end had been so great that contributions towards the new Cricket Pavilion Fund were pouring in, and he hurried over to shake Paddington by the paw.

"I was wondering, bear," he said hopefully, when the applause had died down, "if you would care to turn out for the old boys next year. We're sadly in need of a new swimming pool."

Paddington stood mopping his brow for a moment while he considered the matter from all angles. Although he had enjoyed parts of the game very much indeed the ball had come much too close to his whiskers at times for his liking and on the few occasions when he'd actually touched it it had felt very hard indeed.

In the end it was Alf Duckham who came

to his rescue and decided matters for him. "If you want my advice, bear," he said wisely. "I should retire while you're still at your peak. After all, there aren't many cricketers who can say they've scored an average of fourteen runs a match, especially off one over, and you don't want to spoil a record like that!"

"Perhaps," said Paddington, "I could come down next year and be the interval man."

"The interval man?" echoed the headmaster, looking puzzled.

"I think he means the man who brings the lemonade on during the break," said Alf Duckham. "A most important job. In fact," he continued, voicing everyone's thoughts as he led the way back to the pavilion, "it's such an important job I think you should get a bit of practice in right now. Speaking for myself, a long glass of bears' lemonade would round the day off perfectly."

Chapter Six

A Day by the Sea

Mr Brown stood at the open front door of number thirty-two Windsor Gardens and surveyed the morning sun peeping over the top of the houses opposite.

"Hands up all those in favour of a trip to the sea," he called, looking back over his shoulder.

"People who ask questions like that must expect trouble," said Mrs Brown, after the hubbub had died down and the last of three pairs of feet disappeared hastily up the stairs as their owners went to pack.

"I noticed you and Mrs Bird didn't put up your hands, Mary," said Mr Brown, looking rather hurt. "I can't think why."

"I've been on your trips before, Henry," replied Mrs Brown ominously. "It usually takes me a week to get over them."

"And some of us have all the sandwiches to cut," said Mrs Bird pointedly.

"Sandwiches?" echoed Mr Brown. "Who said anything about taking sandwiches?" He waved his hand grandly in the air. "We'll have lunch in a restaurant. Hang the expense. It's a long time since we had a day out."

"Well," said Mrs Brown doubtfully. "Don't say I didn't warn you."

Anything else she might have been about to say was lost as another clatter of pounding feet heralded the arrival back downstairs of Jonathan, Judy and Paddington together with all their belongings. Paddington in particular seemed to be very well laden. Apart from his suitcase and hat, which he was wearing as usual, he was also carrying his special seaside straw hat, a beach ball, a rubber bathing ring and a bucket and spade, together with a windmill on the end of a stick, a pair of binoculars and an assortment of maps.

Mrs Brown gazed at the collection. "I'm sure they didn't have all this trouble on the Everest expedition," she exclaimed.

"I don't suppose they took any bears with

them," replied Mrs Bird. "That's why. And I'm quite sure they didn't leave a trail of last year's sand on their stairs before they left."

Paddington looked most upset as he peered out from behind his bucket and listened to the remarks. He was a great believer in being prepared for any kind of emergency and from what he could remember of previous trips to the seaside, all sorts of things could happen and usually did.

"Come along everyone," called Mr Brown, hurriedly coming to his rescue. "If we don't make an early start we shall get caught up in the rush and then we shall never get there. A day at the sea will do us all good. It'll help blow some of the cobwebs out of your whiskers, Paddington."

Paddington pricked up his ears. "Blow some of the cobwebs out of my whiskers, Mr Brown?" he exclaimed, looking even more upset as he followed the others out to the waiting car.

While Jonathan, Judy and Mr Brown packed the equipment into the boot, and Mrs Brown and Mrs Bird went upstairs to change, Paddington stood on the front seat of the car and peered anxiously at his face in the driving mirror. There were several pieces of cotton stuck to his whiskers, not to mention some old marmalade and cocoa stains, but he couldn't see any sign of a spider let alone a cobweb.

Paddington was unusually silent on the journey down and he was still pondering over the matter later that morning when they swept over the brow of a hill and began the long descent towards Brightsea. But as they drew near the front the smell of the sea air and the sight of all the holidaymakers strolling along the promenade soon drove all other thoughts from his mind.

Paddington was very keen on outings, especially Mr Brown's unexpected seaside ones, and he stuck his head out of the front window of the car and peered round excitedly as they drove along the front looking for somewhere to park.

"All hands on deck," said Mr Brown, as he backed the car into a vacant space. "Stand by to unload."

Paddington gathered his belongings and jumped out on to the pavement. "I'll find a place on the beach, Mr Brown," he called eagerly.

In the back of the car Mrs Brown and Mrs Bird exchanged glances.

"I know one thing," said Mrs Brown, as

she helped Mrs Bird out of the car. "They might not have had any bears with them on the Everest expedition but at least they had some Sherpas to help with their luggage. Just look at it all!"

"It won't take a minute, Mary," puffed Mr Brown from behind a pile of carrier bags. "Where's Paddington? He said he'd find a spot for us."

"There he is," said Jonathan, pointing to a patch of sand where six deck chairs were already ranged in a row. "He's talking to that man with the ticket machine."

"Oh dear," said Mrs Brown anxiously. "He looks rather upset. I hope there's nothing wrong."

"Trust Paddington to get into trouble," said Judy. "We haven't been here a minute."

The Browns hurried down some steps leading to the beach and as they did so a familiar voice reached their ears.

"Thirty pence!" exclaimed the voice bitterly. "Thirty pence just to sit in a deck chair!"

"No, mate," came the voice of the ticket man in reply. "It's not thirty pence just to sit in a deck chair. You've got six chairs 'ere and they're five pence each. Six fives is thirty."

Paddington looked more and more upset as he listened to the man's words. He'd felt very pleased with himself when he'd found the pile of chairs beside a patch of clean sand but almost before he'd had time to arrange them in a row, and certainly before he'd had a chance to test even one of them, the man had appeared as if by magic from behind a beach hut, waving his ticket machine as he pounced on him.

"Thirty pence!" he repeated, collapsing into the nearest chair.

"I know your sort," lectured the man in a loud voice as he looked around and addressed the rest of the beach. "You sit down in them chairs and pretend you're asleep when I comes round for the money. Or else you say yer tickets 'ave blowed away. Your sort cost the Corporation 'undreds of pounds a year."

The man's voice trailed away as a muffled cry came from somewhere near his feet.

"'Ere," he exclaimed, as he bent down and stared at a heaving mass of striped canvas. "What's 'appened?"

"Help!" came the muffled voice again.

"Dear, oh dear," said the man as he disentangled Paddington from the chair. "You couldn't have 'ad yer back strut properly adjusted."

"My back strut!" exclaimed Paddington, sitting up.

"That's right," said the man. "You're supposed to fit it into the slots – not just rest it on the side. No wonder it collapsed."

Paddington gave the man a hard stare as he scrambled to his feet and undid his suitcase. Five pence seemed a lot to pay just to sit in a chair at the best of times, but when it didn't even have any instructions and collapsed into the bargain, words failed him.

"Instructions?" echoed the man, as he took Paddington's money and rang up six tickets. "I've never 'eard of a deck chair 'aving instructions afore. You wants a lot for yer money."

"I hope you haven't been having any trouble," said Mr Brown, as he hurried on to the scene and pressed something round and shiny into the man's hand.

"Trouble?" said the ticket man, his expression changing as he felt the coin. "Bless you no, sir. Just a slight misunderstanding as yer might say. Tell you what, guv," he continued, turning to Paddington and touching his cap with a more respectful air, "I know these days out at the seaside can come pretty expensive for a young bear gent what's standing treat. If you wants to get yer money back and make a profit into the bargain your best plan is to keep a weather eye open for Basil Budd."

"Basil Budd?" repeated Paddington, looking most surprised.

"That's right," said the man, pointing towards a large notice pasted on the sea wall. "He's in Brightsea today. It's one of them newspaper stunts. The first one as confronts 'im and says 'You're Basil Budd' gets five pound reward. Only mind you're carrying one of 'is newspapers," he warned. "Otherwise 'e won't pay up."

So saying, he touched his cap once more and hurried off up the beach in the direction of some new arrivals, leaving the Browns to arrange themselves and their belongings on Paddington's patch of sand.

Mr Brown turned to thank Paddington for standing treat with the deck chairs but already he had disappeared up the sand and was standing gazing at the poster on the sea wall with a thoughtful expression on his face.

The poster had the one word SENSATION written in large, red capital letters across the top. Underneath was a picture of a man in a trilby hat followed by the announcement that Basil Budd of the *Daily Globe* was in town.

The smaller print which followed went on to explain all that the deck chair man had told them. It took Paddington some while to read all the poster, particularly as he read some of the more interesting bits several times in case he'd made a mistake. But whichever way he read the notice it seemed that not only was Basil Budd anxious to give away five pound notes to anyone who confronted him, but that his own seaside outing would be ruined if he had so much as one note left at the end of the day.

"Good heavens!" said Mr Brown, as he glanced up the beach again. "Paddington is lashing out today. He's bought himself a newspaper now!"

"I pity the person who happens to look anything like Basil Budd," said Mrs Bird. "I can see there'll be some nasty scenes if they don't pay up."

Mr Brown wriggled into his costume. "Come on, Paddington," he called. "It's time for a bathe."

After taking one last look at the poster Paddington turned and came slowly back down the beach. Although he'd been looking forward all morning to a paddle he was beginning to have second thoughts on the matter. Paddington liked dipping his paws in the sea as much as anyone but he didn't want to run the risk of missing five pounds reward if Basil Budd happened to stroll by while his back was turned.

"Perhaps he's having a paddle himself," said Mrs Bird helpfully.

Paddington brightened at the thought. He took out his opera glasses and peered through them at the figures already in the water. There didn't seem to be any sign of a man wearing a trilby hat, but all the same a moment later he climbed into his rubber bathing ring and hurried down to the water's edge clutching the copy of the *Daily Globe* in one paw and his suitcase in the other.

Mrs Bird sighed. Paddington was just too far away for her to make out the expression on his face, but she didn't at all like the look of the little she could see. From where she

was sitting some of the stares he was giving passers-by seemed very hard ones indeed.

"Why can't we have a nice quiet day at the sea like any normal family?" she said.

"At least it keeps him out of mischief," replied Mrs Brown. "And we know where he is which is something."

"That's not going to last very long," said Mrs Bird, ominously, as she watched Paddington splash his way along the shore in the direction of the pier. "There's plenty of time yet. You mark my words."

Unaware of the anxious moments he was causing, Paddington plodded on his way, pausing every now and then to compare the picture on the front page of his paper with that of a passer-by.

The beach was beginning to fill up. There were fat men in shorts, thin men in bathing costumes, men of all shapes and sizes; some wore sun hats, some caps, others coloured hats made of cardboard, and once he even saw a man wearing a bowler, but as far as he could make out there wasn't one person along the whole of the Brightsea front who bore any resemblance to Basil Budd.

After making his way along the beach for the third time Paddington stopped by the pier and mopped his brow while he took another long look at one of the *Daily Globe* posters.

It was a strange thing but somehow with each journey up and down the beach the expression on Basil Budd's face seemed to change. At first it had been quite an ordinary, pleasant sort of face, but now that he looked

at it more closely Paddington decided there was a mocking air about it which he didn't like the look of at all.

With a sigh he found himself a quiet corner of the beach and sat down with his back against a pile of deck chairs in order to consider the matter. Taken all round he was beginning to feel very upset at the way things were going. In fact, if he could have found the man who had sold him the newspaper he would have asked for his money back. But with every minute more and more people were streaming into Brightsea and the chances of finding the newspaper seller, let alone Basil Budd himself, seemed more and more remote.

As he sat there deep in thought Paddington's eyelids began to feel heavier and heavier. Several times he pushed them open with a paw but gradually the combination of a large breakfast, several ice-creams, and all the walks up and down the sand in the hot sun, not to mention the distant sound of waves breaking on the sea shore, grew too much for him, and a short while later some gentle snores added themselves to the general hubbub all around.

Mrs Brown heaved a sigh of relief. "Thank goodness!" she exclaimed, as a small brown figure came hurrying along the promenade towards them. "I was beginning to think something had happened to him."

Mr Brown removed his belongings from the only remaining chair at their table. "About time too," he grumbled. "I'm starving."

In order to avoid the crowds the Browns had arranged to meet for an early lunch on the terrace of a large Brightsea promenade hotel, and all the family with the exception of Paddington had arrived there in good time. Paddington had a habit of disappearing on occasions, but very rarely at meal times, and as the minutes ticked by and the other tables started to fill up, the Browns had become more and more worried.

"Where on earth have you been?" asked Mrs Brown, as Paddington drew near.

Paddington raised his hat with a distant expression on his face. "I was having a bit of a dream, Mrs Brown," he replied vaguely.

"A dream?" echoed Mrs Bird. "I should have thought you had plenty of time for those at home."

"This was a special seaside one, Mrs

Bird," explained Paddington, looking slightly offended. "It was very unusual."

"It must have been," said Judy, "if it made you late for lunch."

Mr Brown handed Paddington a large menu. "We've ordered you some soup to be going on with," he said. "Perhaps you'd like to choose what you want to follow…"

The Browns looked across at Paddington with some concern. He seemed to be acting most strangely. One moment he'd been about to sit down quietly in his chair, the next moment he had jumped up again and was peering through his opera glasses with an air of great excitement.

"Is anything the matter?" asked Mr Brown.

Paddington adjusted his glasses. "I think that's Basil Budd," he exclaimed, pointing towards a man at the next table.

"Basil Budd?" echoed Mrs Brown. "But it can't be. He's got a beard."

"Basil Budd hasn't," said Jonathan. "I've seen his picture on the posters."

Paddington looked even more mysterious. "That's what my dream was about," he said. "Only I don't think it was a dream after all. I'm going to confront him!"

"Oh dear," said Mrs Brown nervously, as Paddington stood up. "Do you think you should?"

But her words fell on deaf ears for Paddington was already tapping the bearded man on his shoulder. "I'd like my five pounds, please, Mr Budd," he announced, holding up his copy of the *Daily Globe*.

The man paused with a soup spoon halfway to his mouth. "No, thank you," he said, looking at the newspaper. "I've got one already."

"I'm not a newspaper bear," said Paddington patiently. "I think you're Basil Budd of the *Daily Globe* and I've come to confront you."

"You've come to confront me?" repeated the man, as if in a dream. "But my name isn't Budd. I've never even heard of him."

Paddington took a deep breath and gave the man the hardest stare he could manage. "If you don't give me my five pounds," he exclaimed hotly, "I shall call a policeman!"

The man returned Paddington's stare with one almost as hard. "*You'll* call a policeman!" he exclaimed. "If you don't go away, bear, that's just what I intend doing."

Paddington was a bear with a strong sense

of right and wrong and for a moment he stood rooted to the spot looking as if he could hardly believe his eyes, let alone his ears. Then suddenly, before the astonished gaze of the Browns and everyone else on the hotel terrace, he reached forward and gave the man's beard a determined tug with both paws.

If the other occupants of the hotel were taken aback by the unexpected turn of events the man with the beard was even more upset, and a howl of anguish rang round the terrace as he jumped up clutching his chin.

Paddington's jaw dropped open and a look of alarm came over his face as he examined his empty paws. "Excuse me," he exclaimed, raising his hat politely. "I think I must have made a mistake."

"A mistake!" spluttered the man, dabbing at his lap with a napkin where a large soup stain

had appeared. "Where's the manager? I want to see the manager. I demand an explanation."

"I've got an explanation," said Paddington unhappily, "but I'm not sure if it's a good one."

"Oh, crikey," groaned Jonathan, as a man in a black suit came hurrying on to the scene closely followed by several waiters. "Here we go again!"

"I've never," said Mrs Bird, "met such a bear for getting into hot water. Now what are we going to do?"

Mr Brown sat back in the Brightsea hotel manager's office and stared at Paddington. "Do you mean to say," he exclaimed, "you actually saw a man putting on a false beard behind a pile of deck chairs?"

"There were two of them," said Paddington importantly. "I thought I was having a dream and then they went away and I found I was really awake all the time."

"But I still don't see why you thought it was the man from the *Daily Globe*," said Mrs Brown.

"I'm afraid this young bear got his 'buds' mixed," said a policeman. "Quite a natural mistake in the circumstances."

"You see, he'd stumbled on South Coast

Charlie and his pal," said a second policeman. "They always call each other 'bud'. I think they've been seeing too many films on television."

"South Coast Charlie!" echoed Mrs Bird. "Goodness me!"

"They tour all the south coast holiday resorts during the summer months doing confidence tricks," continued the first policeman. "We've been after them for some time now but they've always kept one step ahead of us. Kept changing their disguises. Thanks to this young bear's description we've a good idea who to look for now. In fact, I daresay there'll be some kind of a reward."

The Browns looked at one another. After the excitement earlier on, the hotel manager's office seemed remarkably peaceful. Even the man with the beard, now that he had got over his first surprise, looked most impressed by Paddington's explanation. "I've been mistaken for a few people in my time," he said, "but never a Basil Budd let alone a South Coast Charlie."

"Trust Paddington to find someone with a beard sitting at the next table," said Jonathan.

The hotel manager coughed. "That's not really so surprising," he said. "There's a magicians' conference on at Brightsea this week and a lot of them are staying at this hotel. You'll see a good many beards."

"Good gracious!" said Mrs Bird, as she looked through the office window. "You're quite right. Look at them all!"

The others followed the direction of Mrs Bird's gaze. Now that it had been mentioned, there were beards everywhere. Long beards, short ones, whiskery beards and neatly trimmed ones. "I don't think I've ever seen so many before," said Mr Brown. "I suppose that's why South Coast Charlie wore one?"

"That's right, sir," said one of the policemen. "It's a good thing this young gentleman didn't try them all. We might have had a very nasty scene on our hands."

"Perhaps you'd care to join me for lunch," said the man with the beard, addressing the Browns as the policeman stood up to go. "I'm a magician myself," he continued, turning to Paddington. "The Great Umberto. I might even be able to show you a few tricks while we eat."

"Thank you very much, Mr Umberto," said Paddington, as the hotel manager hurried on ahead to reserve a table. "I should like that."

Altogether Paddington was beginning to

think it was a very good day out at the sea after all. Although he hadn't managed to win five pounds by confronting Basil Budd he was very keen on tricks and the prospect of having lunch with a real magician sounded most exciting.

"Hmm," said Mrs Bird, as she followed the others out on to the hotel terrace. "We may be having lunch with a magician but I have a feeling that even the Great Umberto won't be able to make his meal disappear as quickly as Paddington."

Paddington pricked up his ears in agreement as he caught Mrs Bird's remark. It was already long past his lunch time and detective work, especially seaside detective work, used up a lot of energy.

"I don't think I shall have many cobwebs left in my whiskers after today, Mr Brown," he announced amid general agreement, as he sat down at the table to enjoy a well-earned lunch.

Chapter Seven

AN UNEXPECTED PARTY

Paddington paused on the stairs of number thirty-two Windsor Gardens and sniffed the morning air. A few moments later, having consulted the Browns' calendar through the banisters, he hurried on his way with a puzzled expression on his face.

There was definitely something mysterious going on that morning and he couldn't for the life of him make out what it was. Unless Mrs Bird had made a mistake when she'd changed the date, which would have been most unusual; and unless he'd also overslept by two or three days, which seemed even more unlikely, it should have been a Thursday – and yet all the signs were Sunday ones.

To start with there was a strong smell of freshly baked cakes coming from the direction of the kitchen and although Mrs Bird occasionally did her baking during the week she was much more inclined to do it on a Sunday. In any case she never made cakes quite so early in the morning.

Then there was the strange behaviour of Mr Brown. Mr Brown worked in the City of London and in the mornings he followed a strict timetable. Breakfast was served punctually at half past eight and before that, come rain or shine, he always took a quick stroll round the garden in order to inspect the flower beds.

On this particular morning Paddington had nearly fallen over backwards with surprise when he'd drawn back his curtains and peered out of the window only to see a very unkempt-looking Mr Brown pushing a wheelbarrow down the garden path.

"I was wondering when you were going to put in an appearance," said Mrs Bird, as Paddington poked his head round the kitchen door with an inquiring look on his face. "I've never known such a bear for smelling out things."

Mrs Bird hastily closed the oven door before Paddington could see inside and then began dishing up his breakfast. "Don't go eating too much," she warned. "We're having a party this afternoon and I've enough to feed a regiment of bears."

"A party!" exclaimed Paddington, looking more and more surprised. Paddington liked parties. Since he'd been with the Browns they'd had quite a number of Christmas and birthday ones, but it was most unusual to have a party in between times.

"Never you mind," said Mrs Bird mysteriously, when he inquired what it was all about. "It's a party – that's all you need to know. And don't go getting egg all over your whiskers," she warned. "Mr Gruber's been invited, *and* Mr Curry – not to mention quite a few other people."

Paddington carried his plate of bacon and eggs into the dining-room and settled himself at the table with a thoughtful expression on his face. The more he considered the matter the more mysterious it seemed. The most surprising thing of all was that the Browns' next-door neighbour had received an invitation, and Paddington decided it must be a very important occasion indeed. Mr Curry often turned up at the Browns' parties but almost always it was because he'd asked himself and very rarely because he'd actually been invited.

Jonathan and Judy were most unhelpful as well. They came into the dining-room to say good morning while Paddington was having his breakfast but as soon as he asked what was going on they both hurried out of the room again.

"It's a special party, Paddington," said Judy, squeezing his paw as she left. "Just for you. But don't worry – you'll find out all about it later on."

Even Mr Gruber quickly changed the subject when Paddington asked him all about it later that morning.

"I think it's meant to be a bit of a surprise, Mr Brown," was all he would say. "And a surprise wouldn't be a surprise if you knew what it was."

Before any more questions could be asked Mr Gruber hastily broke a bun in two and gave one half to Paddington before disappearing into the darkness at the back of his shop in order to make the morning cocoa.

When he returned he was carrying a large book on the cocoa tray. "I expect we shall be having fun and games this afternoon, Mr Brown," he said, as he handed the book to Paddington. "I thought you might like to have a browse through this. It's a bumper book of party tricks."

Paddington thanked Mr Gruber, and after he had finished his cocoa he hurried back in the direction of Windsor Gardens. Mrs Bird had warned him that with a party in the offing there would be a lot of work to do and he didn't want to be late home. Apart from that Mr Gruber's fun book looked very interesting and he was anxious to test some of the tricks before lunch.

But as it happened all thoughts of party games passed completely out of his mind as he reached home.

While he had been out everyone else had been busy and a great change had come over the dining-room. An extra leaf had been put in the table and the snow-white cloth was barely visible beneath all the food. Paddington's eyes grew larger and larger as he took in the dishes of jelly, fruit and cream, and the plates laden with sandwiches and cakes, not to mention mounds of biscuits and piles of jam and marmalade. In the middle of it all, in a place of honour, was a large iced cake. The cake had some foreign words written across the top but before he had time to make out what they were Mrs Bird discovered him and drove him up to the bathroom.

"You'll have to be at the front door to

welcome your guests," she warned. "You can collect as many marmalade stains as you like this afternoon but not before."

With that Paddington had to be content. But as the time for the party drew near he became more and more excited. The Browns had invited not only Mr Gruber and Mr Curry but a number of the traders from the Portobello Road as well. Despite his habit of driving a hard bargain Paddington was a popular bear in the market and by the time all the guests had arrived the Browns' dining-room was full almost to overflowing.

When the last of the visitors had settled themselves comfortably Mr Brown called for silence.

"As you all know," he began, "this is Paddington's party. I have an important announcement to make later on, but first of all I think Paddington himself wants to entertain you with a few special tricks he has up his paw."

Everyone applauded while Paddington took his place on the rug in front of the fireplace and consulted Mr Gruber's book of party games. There was one chapter in particular which he'd had his eye on. It was called ONE HUNDRED DIFFERENT WAYS OF

TEARING PAPER and he was looking forward to trying some of them out.

"I like paper-tearing tricks," said Mr Curry, when Paddington explained what he was going to do. "I hope they're good ones, bear."

"I think the first one is, Mr Curry," replied Paddington. "It's called THE MYSTERY OF THE DISAPPEARING TEN POUND NOTE!"

"Oh dear," said Mrs Brown nervously. "Must it be a ten pound note? Couldn't you use something else?"

Paddington peered at his book again. "It doesn't say you can," he replied doubtfully. "But I expect I could make do with a five pound one."

"I'm afraid I've left my wallet in my other jacket," said Mr Brown hastily.

"And I've only got silver," said Mr Gruber, taking the hint as all Paddington's other friends from the market hurriedly buttoned their jackets.

Everyone turned and looked towards Mr Curry. "You did say you like paper-tearing tricks," said Mr Brown meaningly. "And it *is* Paddington's party."

Mr Curry took a deep breath as he withdrew his purse from an inside pocket and undid the clasp. "I hope you know what you're doing, bear," he growled, handing Paddington a five pound note.

"Crikey! So do I!" whispered Jonathan as Paddington took the note and after consulting his book once more folded it in half and began tearing pieces out.

The Browns watched anxiously while Paddington folded the note yet again and Mr Curry's face got blacker and blacker at the sight of all the pieces fluttering to the floor.

After a slight pause Paddington took another look at his book and as he did so his expression changed. Whereas a moment before he had seemed full of confidence, now his whiskers drooped and a worried look came over his face.

"What are you doing now, bear?" growled Mr Curry as Paddington hurried over and began peering in his ear.

"I'm afraid something's gone wrong with my trick, Mr Curry," said Paddington unhappily.

"What!" bellowed Mr Curry, jumping to his feet. "What do you mean – *something's gone wrong with it*?"

"The note's supposed to turn up in your ear," explained Paddington, looking more and more unhappy.

"Perhaps it's in the other one, dear," said Mrs Brown hopefully.

"I don't think so," replied Paddington. "I think I must have turned over two pages at once in my instructions. I've been doing the paper doily trick by mistake."

"The paper doily trick," repeated Mr Curry bitterly, as Paddington unfolded the remains of his note and held it up for everyone to see. "My five pound note turned into a bear's doily!"

"Never mind," said Mrs Bird, bending down to pick up the pieces. "If you stick them together perhaps they'll change it at the bank."

"It looks very pretty," said Judy.

Mr Curry snorted several times as he helped himself to a cake. "I've had enough of that bear's paper-tearing tricks for one day," he exclaimed.

Mr Gruber gave a slight cough. "Perhaps you could try one of the other chapters, Mr Brown," he said. "I believe there's a very good one at the end of the book."

"Thank you very much, Mr Gruber," said Paddington gratefully. Mr Curry wasn't the only one who was tired of paper-tearing tricks. Tearing paper, especially banknotes when they were folded, was much more difficult than it sounded, and his paws were beginning to ache.

"There's a very good trick here," he announced after a short pause. "It's called REMOVING A GUEST'S WAISTCOAT WITHOUT TAKING OFF HIS COAT."

"It sounds rather a long trick," said Mrs Brown doubtfully. "Isn't there anything shorter?"

"Nonsense!" said Mr Curry, from behind a plate of sandwiches. "It's a very good trick. I saw it done once years ago in the theatre. I'd like to see it again."

Mr Brown and Mr Gruber exchanged glances. "I'm afraid it'll have to be your waistcoat then," said Mr Brown. "You're the only person who's wearing one."

Mr Curry's jaws dropped. "What!" he exclaimed. "If you think that bear's going to remove my waistcoat you're…"

Whatever else Mr Curry had been about to say was drowned in a roar of protests from the others.

"You said you wanted to see it again," called out the man from the cut-price grocers. "Now's your chance."

With very bad grace Mr Curry got up from his chair and knelt on the rug in front of

the fireplace with his arms raised while Paddington put his paws down behind his neck.

"I thought you said you were going to remove my waistcoat, bear," he gurgled, "not choke me with it."

"Well, it's half off anyway," said Mr Brown, as Paddington pulled the waistcoat over Mr Curry's head until it rested under his chin. "What happens now?"

Paddington put his paw up one of Mr Curry's sleeves and began searching. "I'm not quite sure, Mr Brown," he gasped. "I haven't practised this trick before and I can't see the book from where I am."

"Oh dear," said Mrs Brown, as there came a loud tearing noise and Paddington pulled something out of Mr Curry's sleeve. "That looks like a piece of lining."

"What!" bellowed Mr Curry, struggling to see what was going on. "Did you say *lining*?"

Mr Brown picked up the book of party games and adjusted his glasses. "Perhaps I'd better give you a hand, Paddington," he said.

After a moment he put the book down again and knelt on the rug. "You're quite right," he said, feeling up Mr Curry's sleeve. "It definitely says you should pull the end of the waistcoat down the sleeve, but it doesn't say how you do it. It's very odd."

Mr Gruber joined the others on the rug. "Perhaps if we work backwards it might help," he suggested.

"I think you ought to do something quickly," said Mrs Brown anxiously as Mr Curry gave another loud gurgle.

Mr Gruber studied Paddington's book carefully. "Oh dear," he exclaimed. "I hate to tell you this, Mr Brown, but one of the pages appears to be missing."

Mr Curry's eyes bulged and he gave a loud spluttering noise as he took in Mr Gruber's words. "What's that?" he bellowed, jumping to his feet. "I've never heard of such a thing!"

"I don't think you should have done that," said Mr Gruber reprovingly. "It sounded as though you split your coat."

Mr Curry danced up and down with rage as he examined the remains of his jacket. "*I* split it!" he cried. "I like that. And what was that bear doing at the time, I'd like to know?"

"He wasn't anywhere near," said Mrs Bird.

"I was looking for my missing page, Mr Curry," explained Paddington. "I think I must have used it by mistake when I was practising one of my paper-tearing tricks."

Mr Brown held up his hand for silence. Mr Curry's face had changed from red to purple back to an even deeper shade of red again and it looked very much as if it was high time to call a halt to the proceedings. "I'm sure Mrs Bird can mend it for you later on," he said. "But now I think we ought to get down to the business in hand."

"Here! Here!" echoed a voice in the audience.

Mr Brown turned to Paddington. "Do you know how long you've been with us now?" he asked.

"I don't know, Mr Brown," said Paddington, looking most surprised at the question. "It feels like always."

"Nearly three years," replied Mr Brown. "Which is quite a long time considering you only came to tea in the first place.

"Now," he continued, when the laughter had died down, "we have a surprise for you. The other day we had a telegram all the way from the Home for Retired Bears in Lima. It seems that Aunt Lucy is celebrating her hundredth birthday very soon and the warden thought it would be a nice idea if all her family could be there with her."

"Fancy being a hundred!" exclaimed Jonathan. "That's jolly old."

"Bears' years are different," said Mrs Bird.

"They have two birthdays a year for a start," said Judy.

"Anyway, Paddington," said Mr Brown, "however many years it is, she's obviously very old and it's a big occasion, so we wondered if you would like to go."

"Speech!" cried someone at the back of the room.

Paddington thought for a moment. "Will I have to travel in a lifeboat and live on marmalade like I did when I came?" he asked.

"No," said Mr Brown, amid more laughter. "I've been to see one of the big shipping companies and they've promised to give you a cabin all to yourself this time at special bear rates and a steward who knows all about these things to look after you."

Paddington sat down on his chair and considered the matter. Everything had come as such a surprise and his mind was in such a whirl he didn't know quite what to say apart from thanking everyone.

"I shouldn't say anything," said Mrs Bird. "I should have a piece of cake instead. I've made one specially."

"It's got *bon voyage* written on it," explained Judy. "That means we all hope you have a good journey."

"Come on," said the man from the cut price grocers, as Paddington began cutting the cake. "Let's have a chorus of 'For he's a jolly good bear cub'."

For the next few minutes number thirty-two Windsor Gardens echoed and re-echoed to the sound of singing as Paddington handed round pieces of cake and it was noticeable that even Mr Curry sang, "And so say all of us" as loudly as anyone.

"It'll seem quiet without you, bear," he said gruffly, when he paused at the front door some time later and shook Paddington's paw. "I don't know who'll do my odd jobs for me."

"Oh dear," sighed Mrs Brown, as one by one the guests departed until only Mr Gruber was left. "Everything feels so flat now. I do hope we've done the right thing."

"No more marmalade stains on the walls," said Mr Brown, trying to sound a cheerful note, but failing miserably as Paddington hurried upstairs leaving the others to make their way back to the dining-room.

"I shall leave them on," said Mrs Bird decidedly. "I'm not having them washed off for anyone."

"Well, I think you're doing the right thing," said Mr Gruber wisely. "After all, Paddington's Aunt Lucy did bring him up and if it hadn't been for her sending him out into the world we should never have met him."

"I know what you're thinking, Mary,"

said Mr Brown taking his wife's arm. "But if Paddington does decide to stay in Peru we can't really stand in his way."

The Browns fell silent. When the telegram from Peru first arrived it had seemed a splendid idea to let Paddington go back there for the celebrations, but now that things were finally settled an air of gloom descended over everyone.

In the few years he'd spent with them, Paddington had become so much a part of things it was almost impossible to picture life without him. The thought of their perhaps never seeing him again caused their faces to grow longer and longer.

Their silence was suddenly broken into by a familiar patter of feet on the stairs and a bump as the dining-room door was pushed open and Paddington entered carrying his leather suitcase.

"I've packed my things," he announced. "But I've left my flannel out in case I want a wash before I go."

"Your things?" repeated Mrs Bird. "But what about all the rest of the stuff in your room?"

"You'll need a trunk for that," said Judy. Paddington looked most surprised. "I'm only taking my important things," he explained. "I thought I'd leave the rest here for safety."

The Browns and Mr Gruber exchanged glances. "Paddington," said Mrs Brown. "Come and sit down. You may not have made much of a speech at the party but you couldn't have chosen anything nicer to say to us now. You'll never know what it means."

"I know one thing it does mean," said Mrs Bird. "I can wash those marmalade stains off the walls now with a clear conscience.

"After all," she added, "we shall need plenty of room for fresh ones when Paddington gets back. That's most important."

In the general agreement which followed Mrs Bird's remark Paddington's voice was the loudest of all.

There was a contented expression on his face as he settled back in his armchair. Although he was most excited at the thought of seeing Aunt Lucy again he was already looking forward to his return, and he felt sure that on a journey all the way to Peru and back he would be able to collect some very unusual stains indeed.